HOLDING BEAST

SATAN'S KEEPERS MC
BOOK 7

E.C. LAND

CONTENTS

Acknowledgments	xi
Playlist	xiii
Trigger Warning	xv
Satan's Keepers MC Members	xvii
Prologue	1
Chapter 1	9
Chapter 2	16
Chapter 3	24
Chapter 4	30
Chapter 5	37
Chapter 6	49
Chapter 7	57
Chapter 8	67
Chapter 9	74
Chapter 10	86
Chapter 11	92
Chapter 12	111
Chapter 13	124
Chapter 14	130
Chapter 15	139
Chapter 16	149
Chapter 17	156
Chapter 18	165
Chapter 19	175
Chapter 20	183
Chapter 21	195
Bonus Scene	201
Turn the Page	205
Chapter 1	206

Also by E.C. Land	215
Author's Note	223
Corbin's Conflict	225
Lynch's Match	227
Shiner's Light	229
Striker's Yield	231
Social Media	233

HOLDING BEAST

This book is a work of fiction. The names, characters, places, and incidents are all products of the author's imagination and are not to be construed as real. Any resemblances to persons, organizations, events, or locales are entirely coincidental.

Holding Beast. Copyright © 2024 by E.C. Land. All rights reserved. No part of this book may be used or reproduced in any manner whatsoever without written permission from the author, except in the case of brief quotations used in articles or reviews. For information, contact E.C. Land.

Cover Design by Clarise Tan, CT Cover Creations

Editing by Jackie Ziegler

Formatting by E.C. Land

Proofreading by Rebecca Vazquez

ACKNOWLEDGMENTS

So many people to acknowledge, but first and foremost, my family. They always have my back and support me. My husband and kids are my biggest cheering team, and I couldn't ask for better.

Next, I'd have to shout out to all my readers for sticking with me and enjoying the world I've created.

Then there's my team, everyone who works alongside me to ensure that each book I release is ready to go when the time comes. I couldn't ask for better.

Check out the music playlist for Holding Beast!

Hold On — Torrian Ball
Take This Pain — Jake Banfield
Kiss The Mountain — Auri, Johanna Kurkela
All the King's Horses — Karmina
I Didn't Ask For This — Beth Crowley
Unlovable — DIAMANTE
Used To Be Young — Miley Cyrus
Never Leave Your Guns Behind — Bryan Martin
Where You Belong — Matt Hansen
The Devil in Me — Anthony Mossburg

TRIGGER WARNING

This content is intended for mature audiences only. It contains material that may be viewed as offensive to some readers, including graphic language, dangerous and sexual situations, murder, rape, and extreme violence.
Proceed with caution. This book does entail several scenes that may very well be a trigger to some.
Also, tissues are a must with other scenes.
Not for the faint at heart.
If you don't like violence and cannot handle certain subjects, then this is not a book you'll want to read.

SATAN'S KEEPERS MC MEMBERS

O – OL' LADY & C – CHILD

Reaper - Prez — Ivy – O
Paxton & Sage – C
Angel - VP — Stella – O
Ryland – C
Hellhound - Sergeant At Arms — Isabelle – O
Lucas – C
Daemon - Road Captain — Everleigh
Hendrik – C (Daemon's Son) & Everett – C (Everleigh's Son adopted out)
Hudson – C
Scythe – Tech — Josephine – O
August – C
Tombstone - Enforcer — Sutton – O
Bethany – C (Tombstone's Daughter) & Sebastian – C
Harvester - Treasurer
Thanatos - Chaplain

Styxx - Secretary
Beast – Member – Bristol – O
Ghost – Member
Diablo – Member
Azrael – Member
Cerberus – Member
Serpent – Member
Gizmo – Prospect
Minion – Prospect

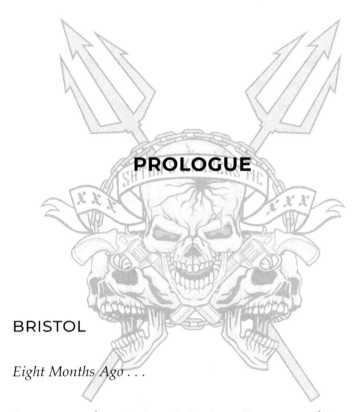

PROLOGUE

BRISTOL

Eight Months Ago . . .

Staring out the window, I don't really see anything out there. I'm not paying attention to the blue sky or the dark clouds rolling in. My mind is screaming at me with all that I'd gone through at the hands of a madman. If not for the pain meds, my body would be throbbing where I was stabbed.

I close my eyes, and my breath hitches as I remember the sound of the guy's voice. Of him telling me he was sorry and that it was my fault because I had allowed myself to be in the wrong place at the wrong time. He hurt me. He raped me, leaving his semen on my body, making me feel dirty than the dirt I laid in.

Then he left me there to die. I wish I had. Dying would have been much more pleasant.

I can't even face those who saved me. The very idea of any of them having witnessed me at my lowest is more than enough embarrassment to handle. I wanted them all to leave, but they refused to go. Ivy, Reaper's ol' lady, has only left me alone to check on the twins. During those times, Reaper sat in the chair, keeping quiet. Even though he hasn't spoken, I've felt his eyes on me. Ivy, though, she's been talking to me every once in a while.

"I want to go home," I finally speak up when Ivy returns, but I don't look at her.

"The doctors don't want you to go home by yourself. You need someone to help you for a little bit while you heal," Ivy remarks, taking her seat next to Reaper.

"I can take care of myself, I'll be fine," I mumble, turning to stare at the two of them. Why is it they won't leave me alone? The nurses were scared to ask them to leave—any of them.

I wanted them all to go, but they refused to listen. That is, all but one.

Beast.

He'd come in earlier, and when I said I didn't want to see him, he turned around and left. From what I've heard, he left the hospital altogether. A part of me aches at the knowledge he did. This being due to the fact I've been half in love with the guy since the first time I met him years ago. But he wouldn't lift the friendship status that he put me in. To him, I was just his friend, along with the waitress who brought him his beers. I had to watch him flirt and take home more than one woman over the course of years.

With this having happened, knowing that I'm in love with the man, I didn't want him to see me like this. It's bad enough he was there when the guys found me. I can't face him now.

"Don't try that shit with us, Bristol," Reaper remarks gruffly. The tone of his voice sends chills down my spine. Put that with the way his eyes seem to hold that edge of rage in them. I've always known he was a man you don't screw around with. Which I wouldn't in the first place. He's a friend along with being my boss. His wife and ol' lady, well, she's become a really good friend. "You need someone to help you, and with all that happened, we're not about to leave you unprotected."

"He's right, Brissy," Ivy says, scooting her chair closer. Reaching out, she takes my hand in hers. "We're taking you home with us. You can stay there as long as you like. You're not alone in this. We're here for you. All of us are."

Not all of them.

Beast wasn't.

But that's my fault.

I turned him away.

And in the process, I feel like I might have lost my best friend.

Four Months Ago . . .

"What do you mean he left?" Pain slices through me at the news Ivy and Sutton just gave me, not realizing the impact it would have on me.

It's been months since the attack, and I'm still living at Reaper and Ivy's house. I haven't gone back to working at the pub, and I don't think I want to. I have a hard time even stepping out the front doors of this house. Going there would be more than I can handle. I finally got to where I can go to the clubhouse without panicking. Going there, I knew I was safe. No one could hurt me there.

Or so I thought.

Beast did, though.

He ignored me the first time I went there and ended up taking one of the women there back to his room.

That was a few days ago.

Now, he's gone.

"Yeah, Reaper, just told me Beast was heading out for a while to handle some club business," Ivy answers, watching me carefully. "He'll be back, though."

I nod, feeling myself shut down. This isn't going to be easy. I've lost him, and I never even had him in the first place.

"You know, Brissy, if you want something or someone, you got to make it known," Sutton remarks, getting my attention with that statement.

"What are you talking about?"

I know I hadn't said anything to anyone about anything that involved Beast.

"Come on, we're not dense. We know you have a thing for Beast. You and he were tight before that day that we shall not speak of," she states, cocking a brow. "That doesn't mean we can't talk about Beast. You want him."

"He left," I whisper, crossing my arms, rubbing my hands up and down my upper arms, trying to get rid of the chill there.

"But he'll be back. When he gets back, all you got to do is hold on and let him know what you want," Ivy says, glancing down to Paxton, who'd run into the room screeching for his mom. His twin sister running behind him with a toy hammer in her hand.

The two of them are hilarious together. They might be toddlers, but Paxton is protective of Sage, even if she's constantly trying to hit him. I love it when Reaper and Ivy let me watch the two kids. In the time I've been staying here, I've become Auntie Brissy to them.

"Sage, stop trying to hit Paxton with your hammer," Ivy mutters sternly, hands planted on her hips.

"But, Mommy, he broke enwine," Sage complains, face getting red as she tells on her brother about him messing up the toy engine she loves to play with.

"Paxton," Reaper calls his son's name as he comes into the room. "I told you about that shit. You don't break your sister's toys."

"She brokes my wegos first," Paxton yells, pointing a finger at his twin.

"Fuckin' hell," Reaper grumbles.

"Reaper," Ivy snaps. "Language."

Sutton and I both snicker because we both know no matter what, Reaper wasn't going to check his mouth around the kids. He says the same thing every time. They know not to repeat the words that come out of his mouth. It's hilarious to watch. That is until he ends up carting Ivy somewhere private.

"I'll just leave you guys alone to hash it out," I state, taking both kids' hands as Sutton follows behind. Thanks to these two kids the conversation was changed from Beast, and I didn't have to hear Ivy say more about it. Hopefully, she won't bring it up again.

"I should probably be getting home too." Sutton

sighs. "I think Tombstone and Bash have had enough daddy-son time to watch football."

"You know you love giving that to them." I smile, happy she has that to go home to.

"Yes, I do, but I also like to be with them to watch the game," she says, grinning brightly. "Anyway, before I go, just think on something for me until Beast gets back. He's the one you want. Always has been, and if you want to keep him, you need to hold on and show him just that. That you're willing to hold on. You've been through hell with what happened. But remember one other thing while you think on this, Beast didn't get his name for nothing. None of them do. Something made him into who he is. See if you can convince him you want him to hold on just as tight as you want to hold him."

Sutton doesn't give me a chance to respond to her words as they sink in. Instead, I watch her leave the room, those words taking root. I want to think about it, but right now, I can't. Honestly, there's no point dwelling on it at the moment. Not when he's gone, and I'm here. Maybe when he comes back, it's not like I'll be going anywhere anytime soon. I'll use the time to finish healing. Hopefully, the two of us can get back to at least being friends like we were.

CHAPTER 1

BEAST

Present Day . . .

There's nothing better than pulling up to the clubhouse after months of being away. Going out on the road was good for me to clear my head. I was also able to use the time to look in locations where the Scarlet Needles could be found. From everything that I've learned and relayed to my brothers, the organization isn't far from home. Those who are involved are just keeping themselves shielded away to keep us from finding them. But we're close to doing just that. I know it deep in my gut we'll get them. We just have to keep at it until we draw them out.

The club's not about to let them get away with

putting contracts out on the women. From what I've heard thus far, nothing's happened while I've been gone, and now that I'm back, I can hope that it stays that way.

I park my bike, slide the kickstand down, swing my leg over and get to my feet. I reach up and take my helmet off, happy not to have to wear it anymore. At least not until I leave the state again. Stepping to the back of my bike, I pull my pack out, throw it over my shoulder, and head for the doors of the clubhouse.

I'm ready to get something to eat, a beer, and find one of the PPs to fuck. Then, I'll find out what else I've missed while out on the road.

What I don't do and have been pushing to the back of my mind is think of a certain woman who, before I left, haunted me. If I'm honest, she still does, but I just shut the thoughts down as soon as they start up. The last thing I need is to bring up the thought of a woman that isn't for me.

We'd been friends before. I'd set that line because she worked at Keeper's Pub, and the club's got a rule. We don't fuck with employees, it's bad for business. But that doesn't mean I didn't want her. I ended up fucking any woman who slightly resembled Bristol just to keep from giving in to my need for her. That was all before she'd been raped and nearly killed.

Bristol was lucky we found her when we did.

Seeing her in the dirt, covered in the blood and semen of another man, it's a sight I'll never get out of my head. To make it worse, she refused to see me at the hospital after we saved her. If Reaper and Ivy didn't demand she all but move in with them, she would have refused help from anyone.

I know the way I handled the situation is probably pathetic, but she made it clear when she wanted me to leave her room that day. Other than the day I saw her before leaving the clubhouse for the past several months, I haven't even heard a word about her, which has helped me overcome my anger and self-pity.

Gripping the handle of the front door, I shove the thoughts of Bristol back down, pull the door, and step over the threshold. As I do this, I'm met with cheers and shouts from my brothers, welcoming me home. I grin at them and move forward to embrace them all. Damn, it's good to be home. I've got to say I did miss being with my brothers and having the camaraderie that we all share.

"Damn glad to have you back home," Diablo says, laughing, that shit-eating grin of his in place.

"Glad to be home."

"Come on, let's get you settled in," he says, slapping my back while Harvester, Ghost, and Thanatos all greet me.

Reaper and Angel step up to me, their women on their arms.

Reaper drops his hold around Ivy and steps toward me. "You get tired of being on the road finally and decided to come home?" He chuckles.

"It was time to come home," I state, shrugging. "Missed all the cooking the ol' ladies do around here. Diner food just doesn't cut it."

"It's a good thing we made your favorite then," Ivy remarks, giggling and snuggling into Prez once again.

"Beef brisket?" The very thought of it already has my mouth watering.

"You got it," Stella pipes in. "We also made pasta salad, the one with the pepper jack cheese, jalapeños, and cut-up salami mixed in. It's our way of saying we're glad you're home."

"Thank fuck, you women," I say, faking a dire face of need. "I don't know what I'd do without you all."

"Maybe you won't take off for months on end again, just remember that," Ivy snorts.

"I'll see what I can do." Chuckling, I turn my attention to Reaper. "I'm gonna head to my room, set my shit down, and be back out here."

"Take your time, brother," Reaper says, giving me a chin lift.

Nodding, I step pass them and start toward my room, only to have my steps faltered at the sight of

Bristol. She's standing there, eyes on me, watching me wearily.

What the fuck is she doing here?

"The ol' ladies asked her to come to the clubhouse," Diablo says quietly from my side. I didn't even realize he'd caught up with me. "She's better with each day that passes. Even moved into her own place again and is back to working."

"Good," I grunt and make my way to my room, shaking off the sight of Bristol here at the clubhouse. "Glad she's back to working at the pub and back on her feet." With her working there, I don't have to worry about my need for her and her refusal.

"Didn't say she was working at the pub," Diablo says as we approach my room.

"Where's she working then?" I ask before I can stop myself. I'm trying not to care about her, but it's not easy. Seeing her was like ripping the Band-Aid right off.

"From what I hear, she's working at some office in town for a hot shot lawyer," he answers.

I open my door and step inside, curious as to what lawyer he's talking about. There are only so many that are in our area. One of those law firms is on retainer with us. The others I don't know too much about.

"Guess that's cool." I try not to let this get to me. "Did anyone look into the firm she's now working at?"

"You know Styxx and Scythe did." Diablo keeps his voice calm and cool, as he always does. No one has ever known him to be otherwise. That is unless you get on his bad side. Only then do you feel his wrath, and that's not something anyone wants to deal with, not even us, his brothers.

Fuck that.

"What did they find out?" Again, I ask the damn question though it's none of my business.

"Clean as a whistle. Hot shot that he is doesn't have any type of record. Well, I should say on the illegal factor. He's a playboy, though, and loves the women. On the front of society papers with a different woman on his arm each time."

This is something I definitely don't want to hear. The very thought of her on the arm of any man pisses me off. In the time I've known her, I never saw her with a man. Then again, we kept our friendship at the bar, so I never asked her about her love life. I didn't want to fucking know anything about it.

"Right." I grunt and toss my bag next to my bed. "Let's get back out there. I'm ready to drink and get shit-faced, then find someone to fuck." Someone not Bristol. She's off limits. No matter what.

Bristol might be over what happened to her, and she's moved on. She also made it clear as fuck about where I stand. I also know that if it were any other way and she didn't turn me away when she did, we'd still be where we are because I know she'd never be able to handle the shit of my past. My demons made me who I am. I just need to stop thinking about the woman who I've dreamed about, who has haunted me as she has for so long, and move the fuck on.

If anything, find a piece of ass to fuck her out of my system. It's high time that happens before I end up doing something I'll regret.

CHAPTER 2

BRISTOL

I knew coming here was a bad idea. A very bad idea.

The moment Beast stepped into the clubhouse, my heart felt like it was going to burst right out of my chest with how fast it started beating. I didn't find out until I got here that he was coming home, and that's why I was invited. If I'd known ahead of time, I wouldn't have come, and I think the girls knew it.

After Beast spotted me, I knew I was right in thinking it was a bad idea and decided it was time to make my escape. The last thing I want to see is Beast getting cozy with one of the slutty skanks that hang around here. Already I've heard a few of them mention how they've missed him and his big dick. I don't need to hear any more or witness what might happen tonight. The ol' ladies had said plenty about the parties in the past, and I definitely don't want to partake in any of it.

Making my excuses, I rush out of there before he has to see me again.

Months ago, Sutton had told me to think about something, and I shoved it aside for the time being. I didn't want to think about it. I couldn't if I had to, I was afraid I'd end up hurt more than I was. It's bad enough that he didn't care enough to fight me when I didn't want to see him after what happened. I still can't talk about it. If I'm honest, it still gives me nightmares. The whole situation. All of it. From the part where I'd been taken, raped, and nearly killed to the part where Beast and the guys found me and, lastly, what happened at the hospital.

I didn't want him to see me like that. I felt embarrassed by what happened to me. I know he did what I asked, but that didn't mean it didn't hurt. He hurt me by showing me how little he did care.

It might sound childish as hell. For that matter, it sounds totally pathetic and makes me seem like a self-absorbed bitch who doesn't think about anything but herself, but considering the way I was raised, I guess you can say old habits die hard.

See, my parents were well-to-do society, and my mother was all about herself. She was more about her spa days and going to the country club. My dad, though, more or less had his head on his shoulders. It's what made him good at being a lawyer. They both came from money, my dad more so than my mom, and they expected me to be a certain way. Well, mostly.

Mom wanted me to find a man, marry, and be like her. My sister followed in her footsteps, and I saw how it turned out for her. No thanks. I don't want that for me. Dad, on the other hand, did demand we have an education and that we learn how to manage things on our own. You could say I took after him in a lot of ways, same as my big brother, but Mom made sure I was still a bitch.

In high school, that's when I learned to fight to be like her. I saw for the first time what she was truly like and decided to change.

Now, I don't really talk to her unless it's at a dinner that my father requests me to attend. For the most part, I can avoid less important ones, but for the others, I have no choice. Needless to say, it wasn't easy when he needed me to come to them during this past year. They didn't know what happened to me. I wanted to keep it that way. The only ones who know who my family is are the ol' ladies and Reaper.

Reaper didn't want to keep it quiet from his brothers, but I explained to him I didn't want them to know where I came from. That's not me. Not anymore.

I might have a trust fund, but it doesn't mean I touch it. I hate being from money. Still, some of the habits I was raised with aren't something easily shaken.

I shake the thoughts away, not wanting to think about any of that. It's a secret I'll keep because I don't want anyone else to find out, for instance, Beast.

Releasing a sigh, I rush to my car, get in, start her up, and get the hell away from the clubhouse as fast as I can.

I pull up in front of my little house on the other side of town. It's technically not small. It's a beautiful three-bedroom ranch-style house on two acres of land with a living room, den, open kitchen, and dining area. The garage is set off to the side and is big enough for two cars.

Reaper and Angel helped me go over it when I wanted to buy it. They made sure that the foundation was good and that I wasn't going to get ripped off in the process of buying it. After moving in I got a job because I used up my savings to put the down payment on my place rather than the trust. I could have easily paid outright, but I didn't. This house is mine. I worked hard and saved everything I could to be able to afford it, and I'm proud of myself for being able to do just that.

My parents live in Dallas, and when I told my dad about buying my house, he seemed proud of me. He even came out a week after I moved in and checked it out. Thankfully, he came without my mom. If she'd come, she'd have found something to fuss about. Probably claimed it was too small or too homey rather than sophisticated as the one I was raised within. Dad thought it suited me, and he was happy I was happy.

Parking in my garage, I grab my stuff and get out. I sigh and make my way up and into the house. I smile as I'm greeted by Jagger, my Maine coon kitty. He was a housewarming gift to me by my dad. He said I needed someone to come home to and that he knew I always wanted one.

"Hey, Jagger," I coo as I set my things down on the table I keep near the door, toe off my shoes, and pull my jacket off. "You want your treat, don't you?"

Jagger always loves getting his treats. He's only fourteen weeks old, and he's already spoiled.

Every day before I leave for work, he gets his breakfast. When I get home, he gets a treat, and later on, I give him his dinner. On days that I leave to go run errands, he gets a couple extra treats. I know it's my fault for spoiling him, but I can't help it. I love the cat. He's got those blue eyes with black and gray fur. He's adorable.

Meowing, he wraps himself around my ankles in answer.

"All right, baby, I'll get you your treat." Laughing, I make my way through the house to where I keep his stash, pull him out several nibbles, and squat down for him to eat out of my hand. Once he's done, I pick him up into my arms. "Tonight, sucked." I sigh, rubbing my nose against the top of his head. "He came back this evening, and he didn't seem happy to see me."

Jagger meows and starts purring.

"Come on," I say, shuffling around the house with him in my arms and heading to the bedroom. It's the weekend, and I don't have to be at work tomorrow, but I have errands to run.

It's different working at a law firm as the assistant to one of the hotshot lawyers who is known for his bachelor ways. The good thing about working for him is he has ethics and doesn't hit on me at work. That doesn't mean he hasn't expressed his interest in connecting outside of work and respected my rejection as what it should be. But he knows who I am and what family I come from. There's no hiding it, considering his family runs in the same circle.

Flopping back on my bed, I curl up on top of the covers and stare into space, unable to keep my thoughts from shifting from my boss at work to that of Beast. It's not hard to do. Beast is the man I've always wanted, and he put the friendship rule in place.

God, seeing him tonight reminds me of what I wanted before that day.

I squeeze my eyes shut and try to shove the memory back down. It's what I've done every day for a while now. To get past it, I try to forget all of it. At least for a while each day. At night, it's harder. I don't sleep for long. If I do, the nightmares come and haunt me. Those nightmares are filled with images of Potter, the man who hurt me, and Beast leaving me. Sometimes my mind plays tricks on me and mixes my desire for Beast with everything else, making things confusingly worse.

There's not really a way to explain it to anyone for it to make sense. At least to anyone other than me.

Now that I've seen him again, that feeling of hurt is back in full force, and I don't know what to do with it. I ache for him, and I've never even been touched by him in any other way than a simple hug every once in a while. Most of the time, it was a fist bump.

I need to simply forget about him and move on. I

shouldn't dwell on the past. It's time to move forward. I've gotten myself a place to live. A new job. A kitty that I love. I just need to get past the pain of what I've been through, and I'll be good.

But how do I do that when all I want to do is hold on to the one man I can't have, nor does he want me.

CHAPTER 3

BEAST

Sometimes, it just pays off to get up in the morning, especially after spending a weekend partying with my brothers. Being away for as long as I was, it felt damn good catching up with them. The PPs didn't even play a part in the weekend. Other than the first night where I imagined it was Bristol on her knees with her mouth around my dick. I was barely able to keep a hard-on long enough to get off. I figured the rest of the weekend, I'd get shit-faced and shoot the breeze with my brothers. We ended up going to the strip club to watch the girls on stage Saturday night, and on Sunday, I stayed at the clubhouse drinking and playing poker along with Diablo and a few others.

I shouldn't have drank all weekend. Not when I

knew I needed to be up first thing this morning. I told Ghost I'd come to the garage and help out. We've got a large shipment of cars that need to get ready to go out and we're slammed with legit work there as well. He needs all hands on deck in order to get shit done.

With my head pounding, I shut off the alarm on my phone, throw the covers off me, ignore the hard-on I'm sporting, and get out of bed. I make my way to my bathroom and step in the shower before turning on the water. I bite back the curse as the cold water wakes me the hell up. Standing under the water, I let it rain over me as it heats up, my eyes closed.

There's not much I can do about the headache other than suffer through it. Washing up, I finish my shower without stroking my dick like I'm tempted to.

Friday night, after dropping my shit off in my room, I wasn't surprised to find Bristol took off. But I didn't miss the fact the ol' ladies weren't happy about it. I'm getting the sense they were hoping to play matchmaker, and that shit's not about to happen. Not with Bristol, or anyone else.

Shutting the water off, I step out and grab a towel to dry off. Finishing the rest of my routine, I get dressed. Once ready, I grab my keys and leave the room in search of coffee. Caffeine will go a long way in helping this headache. If it doesn't, it'll make for a long day working in the garage.

"Yo, Thanatos," I call out from where I was working under the hood of a car. So far, from what I'm finding, there's nothing wrong. But it's got a check light on, and Reaper asked me to take a look at it after bringing it in. "Can I get a hand over here? Need you to turn the key for me."

"Yeah, give me a sec," he shouts back over the music and sound of air-compressed tools being used. A moment later, his shadow comes over as he moves toward the driver's side and slips in behind the wheel. "You ready?"

"Turn the key." The car cranks over smoothly. "Alright, you can stop," I yell and straighten. I decided just to pull the diagnostic reader out and see what that says. I was hoping it would be something simple I could see or hear, but I guess it's not going to be that way.

"What are you doing working on Bristol's car?" Thanatos's questions, causing me to still and look at him.

"This is Bristol's piece of shit car?" It's not a total piece of shit, but it's also not the same one she used to have.

"Yeah, she sold her car to make it more affordable when she bought her house," Thanatos states, shrugging. "This car has been nothing but a nightmare since she got it. One thing after another." He keeps talking, but I'm stuck on the fact she bought her a house. I knew she'd moved back out, but I guess I didn't realize she'd gotten a house. I figured she'd have gotten an apartment or something with the way Diablo talked about it.

What the fuck is she doing buying a house if she knows she can't afford it and the car she did have?

"Last time I looked at it, and I can say this," Thanatos says, moving to lean against the toolbox off to the side. "This car has new brakes, calibers, and spark plugs. We've changed the tire rod-ins, shocks, all the filters, flushed the radiator and oil."

"Is that all?" I grumble, narrowing my eyes on the other man.

"Oh, and air intake has been changed out."

"Right." I shake my head and sigh. "Guess I better get to it and find out what the hell else could be wrong with the damn thing. Is she picking it up here or what?"

"Don't know."

Great.

Without responding, I move in behind the wheel and find the port I need to plug in the scanner under the steering wheel. I go through the process and grit my teeth together when I see what the scanner says.

Misfire on several spark plugs. If this piece of junk just had new ones put in, then it could be the coils are going bad. It's not a hard fix, just a pain in the ass.

Muttering a curse, I get to it, hoping to get done and out of here before she arrives. I don't need to be around when she comes in for it. I've got other shit that needs to be taken care of. Like maybe finding a bitch who I can use to fuck Bristol out of my system. If I were a total dick, I'd go straight to the woman herself and make it happen. But I've gotta feeling that if I were to do that, I'd end up fucking up because I'm pretty sure there's no getting her out from under my skin. She's burrowed in there pretty damn deep.

By the time I finish working on Bristol's car, I'm ready to burn the bitch or blow the damn car up. It's been nothing but a pain in my ass. It's the end of the day, and I wanted to be out of here before she came to get her damn vehicle.

And it looks like that's not going to happen.

"Bristol's car all fixed?" Ghost asks, wiping his hands on one of the grease rags.

"Yeah, the damn thing's done," I grumble, slamming the hood back down.

"Good, 'cause that lawyer she works for is dropping her off."

Great, just what I need. Seeing Bristol as well as her with her lawyer. It's enough to make me want to drink again tonight, and I don't give a fuck about if I get another hangover. It's fucking well worth it not to have to think about her for a little while.

"Right, well, it's ready for when she gets here. Just let me grab the keys from the ignition."

No sooner did those words come out of my mouth a sporty-looking car pulled into the lot. Turning to it, it's all I can do to keep from stepping out there as I watch the car park and both doors open.

My blood turns to ice as my eyes lock with the shit-eating grin on the man's face. A face I haven't seen in years.

My brother's.

"Everett." The name passes my lips on a snarl.

"Well, if it isn't my big brother. Damn if it isn't good to see you, Jarrett."

CHAPTER 4

BRISTOL

Big brother?

I stare wide-eyed between the two men and, for the first time, really see the resemblance. How had I not recognized it before? My boss shared some remarkable resemblances to the man I've wanted for so long.

"Your . . ." I clear my throat and swallow. "You two are brothers?" I ask, unable to keep from staring at them gapingly.

"That we are, Bristol," Everett, my boss, says, nodding as he slowly looks from Beast to meet my gaze.

"What are you doing here, Everett?" Beast growls. The way it comes out it is almost animalistic and somewhat scares me. I've never heard him speak like that.

"I'm dropping my assistant off to get her car. What's it look like I'm doing?" Everett chuckles, seeming to goad his brother.

"Speaking of my car, is it ready?" I ask, more than ready to get the hell out of there. "Jagger's waiting on me."

Both men look at me as I mention my cat's name.

"Car's ready," Beast grunts, "was about to pull it out of the bay."

"I'll just get it myself and get out of here." There's no way I can stick around and listen to more of this.

Finding out my boss is Beast's brother is enough.

I start past them and notice a few other members of the club are watching what's going on out here. Sucking in a breath, I push myself forward and smile at Ghost. "Hey, Ghost, I'm just going to back my car out and head home. Let me know how much the bill is later, will you?"

"Yeah, babe, that's fine. Let me know if you make it home okay."

"I will." Nodding, I get in behind the wheel of my crappy little car and head home, not worrying about anything else. I push thoughts of what I just learned to the back of my mind. I can't think about this. Not now.

Maybe later when I have a glass of wine in hand and am snuggled up to my baby.

It's honestly more than I want to think about even

then, but I'm going to have to process it at some point if I'm going to be able to face my boss again. I knew I should have just taken an Uber to get my car, but he insisted on taking me himself. He claimed there was no reason for me to spend money on a ride when he was capable of dropping me off on his way home.

During the ride, we'd spoken casually, and it wasn't that long of a ride to the garage, which could have made the whole thing weird. It was bad enough I'd already allowed myself to be talked into him driving me in the first place. I can only hope at work tomorrow it's not uncomfortable for me to be around the man who happens to be the brother to the one man I want most.

"Damnit," I whisper, slapping my hand against the steering wheel. I need to stop thinking about all of this.

I drive the rest of the way home, stopping only to grab dinner. I'm not in the mood to cook, and where my house is, there's no way to have anything delivered.

I pull into my driveway, park in the garage, and get out with my food and purse in hand. Off in the distance, I can see the storm clouds rolling in, and the chill in the air sends a shiver down my spine.

My grandmother used to say when you spot the storm coming in, it's just a promise for the trouble ahead. This would be the last thing I need, and I hope there's nothing to it, but who the hell knows. All I can do is hope for the best.

On my second glass of wine, I lay back against the couch. Jagger curls into my side and demands I pet him while we watch *Yellowstone*. I hadn't really gotten into it until recently when I was curious as to what my friends were raving about. It's pretty awesome to watch. I'm definitely a fan of Rip. He's hot. There's just something about him that screams don't mess with me.

I know he's just a character on a TV show, but that doesn't mean he doesn't remind me of a man whose flesh and blood is right here in my very own town.

God knows I'm an idiot where he's concerned.

Halfway through my wine, I hear the sound of a motorcycle and jerk upright. Jagger meows, and I scramble to my feet. No one comes to my house without letting me know first. And the only ones who do come by here know my after-work routine.

Still holding my glass in my hand, I walk over to the door, pull it open, and stare in shock as I watch the man dismount the back of his bike.

His gaze in my direction, and he looks exactly like the name his brothers gave him, Beast.

I don't break eye contact with him as he moves across the distance between us.

My breath catches when he's closer, and I take in the determination on his face mixed with what I can only assume is anger.

"What are you doing here?" I ask with a breath.

"You took off before I could tell you what was wrong with that heap of shit car," Beast mutters, opening the screen door and stepping inside, right in my space.

"That doesn't tell me what you're doing here," I remark.

"I'm here," he growls, wrapping an arm around my waist and yanking me into him. "'Cause I can't get you out of my fuckin' head, and I want to know who the fuck this Jagger fucker is."

I blink up at him, totally taken aback by his admission. "You can't get me out of your head? What does that mean?" A pang twists inside me, and I'm wondering why he would even say that. I mean, he didn't seem to be happy to see me the other night, and he walked away when I needed him the most.

Beast slides the fingers of one hand up in my hair, tangling them in the strands, and keeps me tight with his other arm. "Who's Jagger?"

I blink at him, confused as he dips his head down, getting directly in my face. "Why do you want to know who my cat is?" I shake my head, unable to focus with him so close. "What are you doing here? Seriously, Beast, why did you come here? How did you even find out my address?"

I know the last question is dumb. He could have easily gotten it from one of his brothers. They all know where my house is.

"Your cat?" He furrows his brow, his nostrils flaring.

"Yeah, my cat, Jagger." I shove against him, unsure of what he's doing.

"Your fuckin' cat?" He growls and shakes his head. "Fuck." A breath passes his lips, and he looks ready to explode. "I swear you're gonna do my head in and be the death of me."

I lick my lips, unsure of what he means by that.

Jagger takes that opportunity to break the moment by meowing. Beast looks in his direction and lets me go.

"I should have stayed away," he mutters, more to himself than me, but those words hurt.

"Be my guest and go ahead and leave. There's the door." I raise my arm in that direction, not meeting his gaze. I can't. It hurts too much.

"Said I should have stayed away, not that I was," he growls, pinches my chin, and forces me to look up.

"We've got some things to sort out, you and me. And we're going to do it starting now."

He doesn't give me a chance to respond. I couldn't if I wanted to. Mostly because his mouth was on mine. He was kissing me. His tongue diving into my mouth. It's everything I ever thought a kiss with him would be like and more.

CHAPTER 5

BEAST

I don't know what I was thinking before now. Jealously took hold of me in a way I didn't know how to wash it away without confronting Bristol. More than that, seeing her with my goddamn brother.

Fucking hell.

Scooping Bristol in my arms, I shove all other thoughts from my head for the time being and focus solely on kissing her. I carry her through the house and lay her on the couch, our mouths still fused together. The taste of her kiss is heady, and I want more. So much more.

I break away from her lips and kiss my way down her jaw, her neck, and nip at where her shoulder and neck meet.

"What are you doing to me?" she moans, arching into me, more than obvious she's enjoying my touch.

I slip a hand between us and yank down the tank top she'd changed into. Her tits spill out of the top, and fuck me if my mouth doesn't water all the more at the pretty sight of her nipples. Beaded little nips with hoops pierced through both of them. "When did you get these?" I find myself asking, swiping a thumb over the hardened tip. "I never knew you to have piercings.

"You never really knew me, Beast," she says, her voice sounding almost sad, but it's mixed with arousal. The look in her eyes is the same. One thing about Bristol is she's never been able to hide emotions. Not really.

Except that day in the hospital.

"Think it's past time we remedy that, don't you?" Bending down, I flick my tongue over the tip of her nipple.

Bristol responds with a moan, and I take it as all the encouragement I need to wrap my lips around the hard bud and suck deeply. The noises coming from her spur me on. I take my time enjoying one breast and move to the next using my thumb and forefinger as a way to keep playing with the other.

I want to give her more, and I intend to. That is until the moment is broken by the furious knocking on the front door.

"Bristol, open this door right this minute," a scornful woman shouts.

"Oh my God," Bristol breathes, shaking her head, eyes closed. The way her face pales alerts me to all I need to know, but I do need her to tell me who the woman is.

"Who's at the door, Bristol?" I ask while readjusting her shirt back over her tits.

"My mom," she whispers. "She hadn't been to my house yet."

"I mean it, Bristol," her mom yells, knocking rapidly. "You need to open this door. Right this minute."

"You want her to go away?" Getting to my feet, I pull her up off the couch with me. We're nowhere near done, but for now, it's on pause until we get rid of Bristol's mother.

"I'm not on good terms with her," Bristol finally answers and shakes her head. "You better go. I'm sure whatever she's here for won't be pretty."

"Butterfingers, I'm not going anywhere," I announce, using the nickname she'd earned the first night she started working at Keeper's Pub. That night, she ended up dropping two beers. They slipped right from her fingers and spilled in my lap. Instead of getting pissed at her, I laughed and called her Butterfingers. That was the start of our friendship, and the name stuck all this time. "I'll handle this shit."

"You can't just handle my mom, Beast," Bristol remarks, licking her lips as we ignore the insistent knocking. "You don't know what she's like."

"I guess I'm about to find out then." Letting her go, I quickly stalk to the front door, throw the door open, and stand in the middle of it, blocking the entrance to anyone who dared try to step in. "What?" I demand, meeting the gaze of not just one woman but two, both of which were well dressed in cashmere and pearls. One older, the younger, seemed roughly my age. "Can I help you?"

"Who are you?" Bristol's mother demands, looking down her nose at me.

"Doesn't matter who I am," I grunt, crossing my arms, both women watching as I do this. "I asked what I could help you with?"

"This is my daughter's house. Move out of my way before I have you removed from these premises." The older woman tries to push her way in, but I don't budge.

"Lady, you ain't about to have me removed from Bristol's house, and I ain't moving out of the way until you state your purpose for being here without her knowing you were coming," I inform the woman, realizing she looks somewhat familiar. I just can't put my finger on it.

"Beast, let her in. She won't stop until she gets in here," Bristol murmurs quietly enough for only me to hear.

"You sure?" Glancing over my shoulder, I take in the expression on Bristol's face, seeing she blanked her face, stilling all her emotions.

"Yeah." She nods and moves to pour herself another glass of wine.

That's one thing I knew for sure about her. She wasn't big on beer or liquor, but she loved wine. Red being her favorite. I don't drink the stuff, but that doesn't mean I don't know wines. It's one of the businesses my family dipped their toes into. The winery is my mother's passion, her baby, just as it was my grandmother's.

I shove the thought away before I can end up down that damn rabbit hole. No way do I need to think about anything to do with my family right now. Not until after I get things sorted with Bristol. My brother showing up at the garage the way he did, not only was it to piss me off but he was sending a message. One that was very clear to me. He's going to fuck with me and try and get me back in the family fold. That shit's not about to happen. I left that life for a reason. I don't fit in it and won't return to it. I'm not a hotshot, and I don't do suits and ties. I also don't do conference rooms and board meetings. Fuck that. I prefer to get my hands greasy and handle things with my fists.

I step to the side, and both women outside barge right in, Bristol's mother huffing. Slowly, I close the door, taking in the three women.

"What can I do for you, Mom?" Bristol asks, sounding void of all those emotions I know her to have.

"You can start by telling me why I'm just finding out you bought a house. Then, you can move on to other things. Are you trying to embarrass this family?" Bristol's mother snaps, planting one hand on her hip, the other waving erratically around the space in front of her.

"Mother, calm down," the other woman says, softly holding her fingers in front of her. Eyes cast slightly down in front of her.

"I will calm down once I have answers."

"I suggest you calm your ass down or you'll be back out on your ass, and the cops can see you off the property then," I state, moving from my position at the door to stand next to Bristol and curling her into my side.

The two of us might have issues to work out, but she's not about to take these two on without someone at her back.

"You will do no such thing. This is my daughter's home, and she will not do anything. Considering she used the money from her trust for this house, I have a say in this as I didn't agree to it."

The hell does that mean? Bristol's trust?

"I didn't buy my house with the money from my trust fund, Mom," Bristol announces, sounding annoyed. "I saved to be able to buy my house, and for the record, Dad knows I did this and is proud of me for doing it all on my own."

"Your father is an idiot. He doesn't know what's best for you or this family," the woman snaps, narrowing her gaze. "It's time you come home. I'm done playing these games with you. You have a duty to this family, and I won't see you embarrass us further. Your sister has done as she was told. She married the man we chose for her. Your brother is working and is courting the woman chosen for him. Now, you need to do the same thing and finally accept the proposal and marry the man we arranged for you."

Seems Bristol and I have a hell of a lot more to discuss than I thought.

"You mean the man you picked for me," Bristol snaps. "I told you I will not be doing anything of the sort. I will not live a life where I'm not happy. If that's all you came here for, then you need to leave."

"I will not."

Done with the bullshit, I drop my arm from around Bristol's shoulder and step forward. "Bristol's told you to leave. If you don't, I've already told you what I'll do, and don't think I won't."

"Come on, Mother," Bristol's sister says softly, placing a hand gently on her mother's arm. "We will finish discussing this when you're calm. I'm sure Bristol will listen to reason when we do so."

"Not a chance." I hear Bristol utter sarcastically, but the others don't hear her.

"Fine," her mother sneers. "You best be at the dinner party this weekend." The woman shoots me a harsh, calculating glare and storms out of the house.

Bristol's sister stops at the door and looks back. "Please make sure to come to the dinner party, Bristol. You know how Mother can be. But I promise to try and talk to her. Maybe Dad can talk to her."

"Like you talked her out of the marriage you entered?" Bristol huffs and steps forward. "I can see the bruises you're trying to hide, Giselle. I won't follow in your steps because I know who it is she wants me to marry, and I won't do it. Where your husband only beats you, that best friend of his would kill me, and you know it."

I stiffen at the conversation between the two of them and hate it. I notice the tears in Bristol's sister's eyes and know she knows Bristol is speaking the truth.

"When you're ready to get out of that life, Giselle, you're Bristol's sister, and my club will help you."

Giselle stares at me for a long moment and then looks back at Bristol. "I'll see you at the dinner party," she whispers and closes the door behind her.

Letting out a breath, I shake my head, unable to wrap my head around all this.

"You might as well leave also. I'm tired and ready to go to bed. I don't need any more drama tonight," Bristol states, drains the wine in her glass, turns, and makes her way toward the sink.

With the open space, I can track her movement and watch her ass sway as she walks. Just watching her move has my cock throbbing, but her words just piss me off.

"I'm not leaving, Bristol, so don't try to bullshit emotionless void me," I grumble, stalking in her direction and ignoring Jagger. I still can't believe she's got a cat she named fucking Jagger. I'm not a big cat person, but even I could tell the cat was pretty cool with its intense-looking eyes, even as a kitten still.

A thought hits me, and that hit goes straight to my gut. That day in the hospital, she'd given the emotionless void look to me when she told me to leave, and I fucking did.

It's her shield, and I see that now. I allowed it to fool me when I shouldn't have, and because of it, I've lost enough time. We both did. Then again what time is it we would have had? I refuse to allow someone to deal with what is my past. Hell, my own family doesn't know everything, and they're a part of it.

The only ones to know the truth are my brothers, grandfather, and father. The way I see it, it'll stay that way. I don't want anyone else to know the rest.

Still, when it comes to Bristol, she's under my skin, and there's no working her out. She's in deep, and honestly, I don't know if I want to get her out. Maybe I can have her and keep her from learning everything. Or keep my past from coming for her.

"You need to leave, Beast." Bristol sets her wine glass in the sink and spins to face me, arms crossing under her breast, and the movement pushes them upward. My mouth waters to get my mouth on them again . . . to taste that sweetness I can only imagine between her thighs.

"Not leaving, Butterfingers, so get the thought out of your head. We've got shit to sort out."

"No, we don't," she huffs, shakes her head and drops her arms. "We don't have anything to discuss. I'm nothing to you, and same goes for you."

"That's a fuckin' lie and you know it." I'm not about to let her lie to me or to herself. Closing the distance between the two of us, I wrap an arm around her waist, and my fingers go into her hair, holding her in place. "There's always been something between us, even if we ignored it, Bristol, and I'm not going to let you ignore it any longer."

"You won't let me ignore it?" she whispers, blinks, and narrows her gaze as she presses her hands against my chest and shoves. "Let go of me, asshole." I don't budge, but she doesn't let up, she keeps shoving me. "You've got some nerve saying that to me. It wasn't me who ignored you," she all but shouts.

"Like I said, we've got shit to sort out, and we're doing that starting right fuckin' now," I inform her, letting her hair go and wrapping my fingers around her wrists, stilling her from shoving me further. "Why did you tell me to leave that day in the hospital?"

Bristol stills in my arms, her body going tense. Eyes wide. Lips parting. Her breathing shallow.

"Why are you asking that?"

I don't think she means to ask, but she does, and I'm going to answer.

"Because I didn't want to leave you. I didn't want to leave you alone after what you'd just been through, but you told me to leave, that you didn't want to see me."

Bristol starts shaking in my arms, and I tighten my grip on her, hoping to still the shakes from her body, but it doesn't work. Letting go of her wrists, I scoop her in my arms and carry her through the house.

Without asking her, I find her room and move right to the bed, where I lay her in the middle and stretch out next to her, my arm still wrapped around her.

"Talk to me, Brissy. Why did you want me to leave you?"

"I didn't want you to. Not really. I didn't want you to see me like that. Not after finding me the way you did. I was embarrassed."

I close my eyes and release a heavy sigh, feeling a weight slowly lift off my shoulders. It is one of many things that have sat on me for a long time. That one, though, was a heavy one, and I knew, some part of me damn well knew, that was the damn reason she didn't want to see me. Fuck. If I could go back and kill Porter, I would. The bastard died way too easily. The fire he'd started was meant to kill him and Josephine. He'd been obsessed with her and didn't like that she was my brother's woman. Why he hurt Bristol, I'll never understand, but he hurt her when he couldn't get his hands on Josie, and that alone makes me want to bring him back from the dead and gut him like the piece of shit he was.

For Bristol, thinking of what happened to her as embarrassment guts me, but I can at least fix what I should have done all those months ago rather than walking away the way I did.

CHAPTER 6

BRISTOL

Nervously, I lick my bottom lip, wanting to kick myself for allowing myself to not only enjoy the kiss Beast and I shared a bit ago, which I'm blaming on the wine I've consumed tonight, but also that I admitted what I just did. Again, I'm blaming it on the wine. Otherwise, I wouldn't have done either.

At least that's the story I'll keep telling myself. Otherwise, I might have to admit something else altogether, and I'm definitely not going there. Nope. No way.

The way Beast handled my mother didn't help, and then there's the way he spoke to my sister about helping her if she were ever to decide to finally get out of the hell she's living in. But I honestly don't know if she ever will. My sister is a people pleaser. I don't think she had a chance to be anything else. Or ever will. She's allowed my mother to dictate her entire life, and I don't know why. If I did, maybe then I'd have been closer to Giselle. I might have even respected her rather than kept my distance.

What I don't get is why my mother seems to think that she has any say when it comes to my trust fund. She has no say in the matter. Not now. I'm an adult, and if I wanted to use it, I could. There's nothing in it that says I have to have her permission to use it. Granted, I didn't use it at all, but still, what's it matter to her?

"I shouldn't have left. Should have demanded to stay with you, but I didn't," Beast says softly. "That's on me, and I'll have to deal with it still, I'm not letting it get between us. Not anymore. We've got a lot to go over, and we're not gonna get to it all in one day, which is okay. We've got time. What matters right now is that we talk about it, what the fuck your mother was talking about, and how the hell did you hide the fact you came from money?"

"I didn't hide it." I shrug. "I just didn't talk about it." This is true. The best way to forget about something like this is to just not talk about it. You don't talk about having money, then people won't treat you like you are. I also don't rub my nose at this fact. I would prefer to be broke as dirt than have all the money in the world if it were my decision.

"I get that," he grunts and gives my waist a squeeze. "Now, what did your mother mean?"

"She seems to think she can choose who my siblings and I are to marry. She might have gotten her claws in Giselle, but there's no way Ben or I are doing what she wants. Sure, my brother is working for our dad, but that's because he loves what he does. As for the courting BS, he's told me he's dating a woman that he's actually in love with. According to him, she's funny and makes him laugh. There's no way he'd allow our mother to push a woman on him he doesn't want. Besides, Dad has told all of us that if it's not something we want, then so be it. He's more down to earth, but he does have his moments. Usually, that revolves around financial decisions. Not personal, unless it's something that will reflect on him in a way he wouldn't approve of."

"Like you being with a man from a motorcycle club?"

"I don't think so. He doesn't like my brother-in-law because he knows what's happening to my sister but can't do anything about it due to who the family is," I answer truthfully and suck in a breath. "Our mom wanted to become one of the top families in society, I guess you can say. She's worked at it, making sure that arrangements were made for her daughters to marry powerful men."

"And who does she want you marrying?" he demands, that gruff voice of his turning harsher.

I swallow, turn to my back, and sit up, pulling my knees up to wrap my arms around them. "My sister is married to Ronnie Fisher. She picked Ronnie's best friend for me, Cordell Barker."

"Cordell Barker," Beast mutters at the same time I give the name.

I swing my head toward him, feeling my eyes nearly bugging out. "How did you know that name?"

Beast slowly sits up and scoots to sit with his back to the headboard, arms crossed over that beefy chest of his that I've admired for so long. "I know that name because Cordell Barker is my cousin."

I don't think shock could cover exactly what those words do to me.

"You . . . you're . . . wait," sitting up on my knees, I turn to face him, "you're Cordell Barker's cousin? How's that possible?"

"Cordell's mother is my father's sister. She married Cordell Senior."

Whoa.

This is unreal. How in the world is this possible? Wait!

"I don't get how you're . . . well, related to him. For

that matter, I work for your brother, and I didn't even know it." I still can't believe that one.

"Everett and I are brothers, yes. However, I'm no longer a part of that world. I left it a long time ago, and I refuse to go back to it. I won't be a part of that world."

"Why?" I ask before I can stop myself. "Are you not a part of your family's life at all?" It's the one reason I still go to family things. To see my dad, at least. And my brother.

"No," Beast clips out harshly. "I turned my back on all of them a long time ago, and I have nothing to do with them."

"But it seemed your brother wanted to have something to do with you when he dropped me off." Even in my shock, I saw this.

"Everett can want all he wants, but I'm not going back to that family." Beast narrows his eyes, and my stomach tightens nervously. "And what the fuck are you doing working for the annoying bastard? You fuck him?"

Blinking, I find myself speechless. I open my mouth, but words fail to come out. It takes me a few seconds, precious seconds at that, to find the words. "You have a lot of nerve to ask me that, Beast. For the record, I haven't and wouldn't; however, that's none of your business. I will tell you this, though, your brother is a good guy to work for. Professional and kind. Yes, he's a playboy, but he doesn't cross that line with me. He was kind enough to give me a ride to the garage today to keep me from spending money on an Uber ride."

"Why didn't you just call one of the brothers to come get you?" he asks.

"Because I'm not helpless. I can make my own way." I huff and shake my head.

"Right, and that's why you traded your old car, which was shit, for something that's a hell of a lot shittier." Grunting, he leans forward, grabs my waist, and pulls me over him. In this position, I have no other choice but to straddle his lap.

"What are you doing?" I ask, pressing my hands against his chest.

"Holding you where I want you," he remarks, gliding his hands over my waist. "Now, answer the question about why you're working for my brother."

"Because I didn't want to go back to the bar, and there weren't really any slots available at any of the other places' businesses. Unless I wanted to go to the strip club, and that wasn't happening. I can't dance worth a lick, and I'm not big on being around a bunch of horndogs." I don't bother mentioning that I didn't want to be around a bunch of strange men, not after what I went through. "I feel safe working where I am now. There's security there, and no one comes in unless they have clearance. And they walk me out in the evenings."

"Right," Beast remarks, nodding, his hands stilling in place on my waist. "And this house? You wiped out your savings for it, didn't you."

How did he know that?

"That's what I figured." Shaking his head, he lets out a heavy breath. "You are one stubborn woman, you know that. It's a fuckin' turn on, at the same time, a headache."

"Well, lucky you, you don't have to worry about me being either for you. Now, can you let me go then leave?" I snap, feeling as though he'd insulted me for wanting to do something for myself. I mean, I saved for so long to be able to have this. To not have to worry about a large payment when it comes to my mortgage. I wanted a small one so that I could start saving for a new car. If I keep saving for the remainder of the year, I'll have enough for a good down payment that will also allow me to have a decent car payment. I don't want to be paying out the ass and worrying about my bills.

"Butterfinger, I'm not leaving, but we can finish this discussion later. It's getting late, and we both have work tomorrow. After the day I had working on your car and dealing with other shit, I'm exhausted."

"You're not staying here," I blurt out and try to get off his lap.

"Yeah, I am. Then tomorrow, I'll take you to work. While I'm there, I'll be meeting with my brother to find out exactly what he's playing at."

"You can't do that. Either of those things."

"Why not?" he asks, cocking a brow.

"Because I don't need you to take me to work, and you can't meet with your brother because he's got court in the morning, then meetings scheduled for the remainder of the day." I know Everett's schedule like the back of my hand.

"Then I'll be picking you up after work so that I can take you to dinner," he announces. "But I'm still staying the night, Bristol, so stop arguing and get ready for bed."

Staring into his intense eyes, I know he's not going to budge on this, so I let out a huff and roll my eyes, giving in for the time being.

CHAPTER 7

BRISTOL

Can a man be more annoying than Beast has been for the past week? He's driving me insane. I mean, I can drive myself, but he's refusing to let me drive my car. He claims it's a death trap in the making. All week he's driven me to work, escorted me to my office, came by at lunchtime, and picked me up in the afternoon. My boss found this hilarious when he came in from court yesterday to find out what his brother had been doing.

I want to kick them both, but I can't. I'd probably end up hurting myself in the process.

Every day he's taken me home, the two of us ate dinner together, talked, and he'd make me laugh. We'd end up on the couch, me snuggled into him while he laid on his back, me between him and the cushions.

Most of the time, we ended up making out. He didn't push further than that, like the first time when we'd been interrupted by my mother and sister showing up. Afterward, he'd take me to the bedroom, where we'd sleep.

The one good thing about Beast sleeping next to me is that I haven't had a nightmare. This I thought, was a good thing.

With all of that, I still feel completely confused by him. What's with the sudden change? I don't get it. When we first met, that friend line was drawn between us, and he made it known. He knew that I wanted him, but because of the rules the club has, he never went there. This, I got, doesn't mean he didn't baffle me with his flirting and then giving me the cold shoulder as well.

Now, he's all about touching and being with me, yet there's a part of him holding back. I can sense it. It's in his eyes. The demons there still have hold of him, and I find myself wondering about what darkness lies within his mind.

Tonight's a party at the clubhouse, and Beast informed me that we would both be going to it, but I hate to break it to him, I won't be able to attend. My dad called and invited me to dinner with him and Ben. Said the three of us needed to talk about a few things and said my mother would not be in attendance. I found this confounding, considering the dinner party is tomorrow.

"Bristol, do you have that file for this afternoon's meeting ready?" Everett asks, drawing my attention from the screen to see him standing in the open doorway, leaning against the frame.

"Yes, it's right here," I answer, grabbing the folder he's speaking of and handing it to him. "Also, I'll be leaving early today if that's okay."

"My big brother picking you up like he's done every day this week?" He smirks and steps forward to take the file.

"No, he doesn't know I'll be leaving early, and I'd like to keep it that way. I'm being picked up by a car my dad's sending for me," I retort, refocusing on the computer screen and the schedule I was working on for next week. I'm trying to stay ahead of schedule and make sure I'm ready for the next week.

"Sounds like that should be interesting."

I'm not so sure of that. I want to know what my dad needs to talk to me about, but at the same time, it scares me. It could be about anything.

"Well, this should be interesting then." Chuckling, he heads back to his office. "Have a good time, and I'll deal with my brother. Maybe he'll actually stick around to talk to me." Closing the door behind him.

I stare at the closed door, wondering what he meant

by that. Granted, Beast refused to even speak to my boss. He just hurried me out of there.

An hour passes by, and I close down my computer, grab my things, and make my way down to the front. I'm surprised to find my brother leaning against the back of a black Town Car.

"What are you doing here?" I ask once I'm close enough not to have to shout.

"Dad sent the car for me first at the office, we're evidently riding together. Do you know what this is about?" Ben asks, his brow arches up and over his sunglasses.

"No, just that he wanted dinner with the two of us, and he would send a car for me this afternoon. You haven't spoken to him?"

"Not really, it's been busy at the office, and he hasn't been in this week." Ben steps away from the car and opens the door for me to climb in. He follows suit and closes the door. The moment the doors close, the car pulls away from the curb. "So, tell me how you've been doing. How's living in a house you bought and paid for without using the trust fund?"

"I love my house, Ben, and I worked hard to get it. You knew I wouldn't use the money in that account. I also didn't want to deal with Mom being her typical self, which she came to my house and did Monday night." Rolling my eyes, I cross my arms and settle into the seat cushions as the driver makes his way from my place of work to wherever he's taking Ben and me.

"Oh, trust me, I heard about her coming over and you having a criminal in your house," Ben snorts. "There's something to be said about the way Mom acted and spoke. She was out of her mind, furious."

"Good for her," I mutter on a sigh.

"Yeah, Giselle called me to give me a heads up and warned me to keep Lexie away from Mom. She doesn't know about the two of us yet. Still thinks that I'm courting Vivian." I'm surprised by the fact our sister called Ben and told him this. Why couldn't she have done this for me? Ben reaches for my hand and gives it a squeeze. "Elle also told me what your friend said before leaving your house. She really wants to take him up on the offer, but she's scared."

"Why?" I don't get what she's got to be scared about. She'd be free of the asshole she's married to.

"That's for her to share, Bris, but you know if you were to actually talk to her without looking at her like you were judging her, she might feel like she can talk to you."

Ouch. That hurt.

"I can't help it. The way she is with Mom . . . always by Mother's side, with that husband of hers, constantly ridiculing me, how can I not judge?"

"I see your point as well," he remarks. "It sucks

being the middleman between the two of you. I hate what the woman is doing to both of you. Fuck, I don't even care to be around the insufferable woman, but I do it to be able to check in on Elle. She can't always call me. Ronnie monitors her calls."

"Of course, he does," I scoff. "He's a dickhead with more than enough issues to go around." Before Ben can speak further, the driver pulls into the driveway of a house I don't recognize. "Where are we?" I ask as the driver comes to a stop.

"Don't know but we'll find out," Ben says, opening the door.

As I slide out of the back seat, I spot my dad coming out of the front of the house.

"Ben, Bristol," he calls out, arms open, a huge grin on his face.

"What's going on here, Dad?" Ben demands, getting right to the point.

"That's why I asked you both to dinner," Dad remarks. "Come on in, dinner is on the table."

I look to Ben, and he does the same. Neither of us speaks as we follow our dad into the house. It's not a big house like the one he shares with our mom. It's more homey, lived-in, cozy perhaps. It's more like my house than anything.

The three of us take a seat at the table, and I'm

surprised to find it's all home-cooked food and not something prepared and served to us.

"Did you cook this?" I blurt without thinking.

"That I did." Dad chuckles and starts filling his plate. "I needed to talk to you all, and I figured why not tell you all here."

"You're leaving Mom, aren't you?" Ben asks, cocking a brow.

"I am." Dad nods. "I filed the paperwork yesterday to get the ball rolling."

"Isn't she going to get half of everything?" I ask, worried about what's going to happen to him. He doesn't deserve to be put through a nasty divorce.

"Dad's prenup covers him," Ben answers for him, nodding. "Glad to hear you're finally doing it."

"Wait, I'm confused and feel like I'm missing something," I state, waving my hands wildly in front of me.

"Your mother, when we got married, had to sign a prenuptial agreement, one my mother had drawn up, stating that if there were any reasons for divorce on your mother's part, no matter the circumstances, she would not receive a penny from me. That reasoning could be anything. You know your grandmother was ruthless and made sure to word the agreement so that I would win over her if it came down to it. Your grandmother never really liked your mother as it were."

"Whoa." I lean back in my seat and stare at my

dad, finding it hard to believe what I'm hearing. "So, you've moved out of the house. Are you giving it to her?"

"It's the only thing I'll allow her to have. She won't be getting a dime from me. The only money she'll have is from whatever she has that isn't connected to me. I won't be giving her anything."

"What's the reasoning you're using?" Ben asks.

"I'm using the fact that she's screwing around on me and trying to access control over Bristol's trust fund, claiming she's not of the right mind, which is total bullshit."

"I'm sorry?" I swear I must not have heard him correctly.

"Tell me you're joking," Ben sneers.

"Afraid not." Dad sighs, taking a bite of the fluffy mashed potatoes. "I got a call from one of the other firms to inform me. After I hung up, I made a call to JE Boise."

"You called my boss's dad?" I gasp, eyes wide.

"I did." He nods, giving me a sad smile. "But that's not the JE Boise I'm speaking of. You know him as Beast."

"How do you know Beast?" My dad seems to be full of surprises today.

"I went to school with his father and knew exactly who your mother was ranting about. I called JE, and he gave me his son's number. In fact, he should be here at any time now."

Oh my God. He can't be serious.

"You told him to come here?" I utter, trying to breathe.

"I did. If we're going to protect what's rightfully yours, we need all hands on deck, and that includes Beast and anyone else he brings along with him," Dad states and looks to Ben. "And before you ask, the reason I didn't just tell you to drive over here is because I don't know if your mother is having you watched. She's clearly going out of her mind, and I'm protecting you the best way I can."

"What about Giselle?" I whisper.

"That's being taken care of," Dad remarks, nodding. "As we speak, she should also be on her way here. When I spoke with Beast, I asked him to see to getting my other daughter safely away from her abuser." The grimace that crosses his face hurts me. "I've not done right by the three of you by allowing your mother to control so much. But I intend to fix all of that the best way I can. Your sister called me and said she needed help. Told me that Ronnie beat her for the last time, she couldn't take it anymore. She asked if I could talk to you about getting your friend to help her. I went ahead and asked him myself while I spoke to him."

Guess that would explain why he wasn't at the office during lunch today.

All of this is a lot to take in, and my head is reeling right now.

Sitting back in my chair, I allow all this information to sink in. Everything in my world is changing, and I don't know how to handle it all.

The rest of dinner is done in silence, all of us waiting, allowing everything to set in.

My stomach tightens, thinking about seeing Beast again. Here I thought he, and I would be arguing later when I got home. Instead, my dad asked for him to help with our family issues, and that's not something that I thought would ever happen. Why would he do that? This whole situation is more than I can handle right now.

Finding out everything I have so far, my dad leaving mom, Giselle finally leaving Ronnie, and, of course, my mom trying to claim I'm not in the right frame of mind. God, I can't handle anything else, but I've got a feeling there's more to come.

CHAPTER 8

BEAST

Blood roars in my veins, and I want nothing more than to go back and wait for fucking Ronnie Fisher to get his ass home from work in order to beat the hell out of him the way he did my woman's sister. Fucking hate men like him. I always have. If it wasn't for the fact Giselle pleaded with me to get out of there, I would have. Only days ago, I told the woman I'd help her, and here I am, helping Bristol's sister get free of a motherfucker who is nothing more than a dead man walking, in my opinion.

This morning, I'd been surprised when Quinten Hensley, Bristol's father, called me. I hadn't realized that was my woman's father at first, not until he introduced himself to me. I should have put the names together when I realized she was from money, but I didn't. All I knew was her mother looked familiar, but it'd been years since I was a part of that world.

Quinten asked for my help. At first, I wanted to tell him to go to hell, but he'd quickly explained the situation to me, starting with what Bristol's mother was trying to pull. That shit alone pissed me off. Then he went to expand, and that did the trick. No wonder Bristol is the way she is, her bitch of a mother caused it, and I'm going to remedy that. Draw out the woman who only shows herself when she thinks I'm not watching her.

I know before what happened all those months ago, nearly a year ago, she laughed more. She went to work and had bright eyes. That light went out of them, and I want it back. That's one of the few things I made a decision on this past week. I want Bristol, and I'm going to hold on to her. Even if I'm struggling with my own demons. I made the decision Bristol was going to be mine, and I'm not about to change my mind. She means something to me, and I've always known that; however, now that something has turned into a hell of a lot more.

I'm trying to ease her into what I want from her. That doesn't mean I haven't thought of tasting those pretty nipples of hers again or tasting other parts of her. Having her curled into me at night, her body snug against mine, fuck, it's been hard not to just fuck her when I'm trying to be gentle.

Tonight, we were supposed to be partying at the clubhouse, and I was going to take us further into this. I intended to finally taste that hot little pussy of hers, unfortunately, Quinten called. Now, I'm on my bike, heading to the address he gave me. Diablo, Thanatos, Ghost, Reaper, and Styxx are riding with me while Cerberus is in the van with Giselle.

When we got to her house, she was alone and beaten. Her lip was busted, both eyes black, and her neck, you could see the handprints bruised into her skin there. We loaded her up in the van and got all of her stuff packed in the back. While she sat in the van, Reaper talked to her. Gave her the option to go to a safe house where no one could find her. She said she wanted to talk to her dad first, and I get that. Her dad is going to lose his shit when he sees her like this. But then again, he knew what she was going through and didn't do a damn thing about her. It would do him good to see her like this. To know that he allowed it to escalate to this point. Yeah, he deserves to see her like this.

At the same time, it sucks for him because he's trying, and I can tell none of this has ever set well with Quinten. I don't know the man personally, but my old man does. They'd gone to school together.

They did business together at times when it was beneficial for them both. The old man gave Bristol's dad my number, and the only reason he had it in the first place was because it was in case of an emergency. He hadn't used the number, and I hadn't called him.

Seeing the house and driveway, Quinten gave me the address for, I guide my bike up the driveway and park my bike behind a black Town Car. He'd told me he was having that car pick up both his son and Bristol. He intended to talk to both of them before I got here. He's had his time. Now, I'm going in there, seeing to business, then taking my woman with me. I still have plans for her.

I also intend to have it out with Bristol considering she didn't fucking call me 'cause the last thing she knew was that I intended to pick her up as I have since I took her to work on Tuesday. The two of us are going to get a few things straight, then after that I plan to get that taste of her I wanted to get tonight.

Kicking the stand down, I climb off the back of my bike and straighten my cut. I glance at my brothers to see the grim expressions on their faces. It's also mixed with anger for the way we found Giselle.

I give them a jerk of my chin in acknowledgment and head for the doors as Thanatos moves to help Giselle from the van. Once we get her inside, he'll take a look and make sure she's good, and it's all just superficial and nothing more.

Taking the steps two at a time, I grab the door handle and shove it forward, stepping into the house. I don't bother speaking or announcing myself. I'm sure they all heard my bike. My boots echo in my ears at the silence of the house, and I start to wonder if they're even here when I round the living area and find them all standing around the kitchen counter waiting.

I meet Bristol's eyes and take in her expression. Dropping my gaze, I see the way she draws that bottom lip in between her teeth. She's nervous and rightfully so. I fully intend on paddling her ass later when we get back to her place. Or maybe I'll take her to my room at the clubhouse. There I could enjoy using things I ordered specially for her.

"Beast," she whispers, taking a step away from the counter in my direction. "Did you get Giselle?"

And that right there, even if she doesn't want to, she cares for her sister. I see the pain in her eyes . . . the longing. She wants her sister in her life, but not if it includes her mother. I get that.

"Yeah, Butterfingers, we got her. Thanatos is bringing her in. But you gotta know, baby, she's in bad shape," I answer, tucking a strand of hair behind her ear.

"Thanatos is gonna need somewhere to check her

over," Reaper states, coming to stand next to me, getting Bristol's attention. "Brissy, babe, you've got some explaining to do. Ivy is pissed with you right now, the twins want Aunt Brissy, and you haven't been around."

Bristol rolls her eyes and grins. "Reaper, it's you who's pissed because Ivy's getting on you about cursing in front of Paxton and Sage. I've already heard about Pax repeating you using the 'F' bomb. Because I wasn't there to distract the kiddos, you couldn't take Ivy's mind off what she's mad at you for." She snickers.

"Damn, woman, here I thought you loved me," Reaper states, shaking his head and reaching a hand out toward Quinten. "I'm Reaper, President of the Satan's Keepers MC, and Beast here's my brother."

"Quinten Hensley," Quinten says, taking Reaper's hand. "Nice to meet you. I see you know my daughter well. This is my son Benjamin. I appreciate all of you helping . . ." He slides his eyes to me, not finishing that sentence.

I nod, knowing exactly what he's talking about. Us going after Giselle and bringing his daughter home to him.

Thanatos carries Giselle in with Cerberus right behind. No one says a word as the two men move to the couch, but eyes follow the movement of my brothers. I keep mine on Bristol, watching it hit her exactly what her sister's been going through. I see the guilt eating at her, and I'm not about to let that take root. She's been through enough of her own, and I'm sure none of her family even knows the exact pain and hardship she's dealt with.

As much as I'd prefer to deal with that guilt now, I won't do it. I'll handle it later when it's just the two of us, here alone, with no one around to interrupt how I'm going to get through to her.

CHAPTER 9

BRISTOL

Tonight has been nothing if not the weirdest night of my life. It's like my two worlds, neither ow which I fully belong to, merged together. My family, well my dad, brother, and sister, I guess you can say they're all of my family, considering my mother is definitely not a part of that. Oh no, definitely not. Not after what my dad informed me of. Anyway, my family met some of those I've seen as friends and a few close as family.

There's a small part of me that wants to run and hide, but seeing the way they all fit together, it was nice. Well, except for the part about my sister. That part hurts. If I'd connected with her, talked to her, the two of us could be closer, and she wouldn't have been dealing with all of this alone.

Beast, for the most part, has been distant. Sure, he touched me, but you could tell he was pissed with me. It was in his eyes. In the way he didn't speak. Not to me, other than the initial greeting. Even through the distance he's put there, he's stayed close but not touching. I don't know what to say to him. I feel slightly humiliated that he was pulled into all my family drama. He shouldn't have to be dealing with any of it. It's not his business. I don't want him to have to worry about any of this. It should be my brother and me who handle it all, not Beast or those of the club.

But how would I even know where to begin when it comes to any of this?

I listened to all of them talk throughout the evening keeping quiet. What else can I say? I'm a lousy sister for one thing, so I can't do much there. I hate being here and feeling like an outsider, and I know I did it to myself.

I'm about ready to ask my dad if the Town Car can just take me home when Beast grabs my hand.

"We're heading out," he announces, surprising me. I tilt my head back and stare at him momentarily.

"You going to the clubhouse?" Diablo asks, cocking a brow.

"Nope, we're heading home." Beast pulls me close and wraps an arm around my shoulder. "See you Monday at the shop."

"Sunday," Reaper states. "We've got the family picnic at the clubhouse, brother. You miss it, Ivy, Stella, and the rest of the ol' ladies will be on your ass."

"We'll be there," Beast says.

"See you then," Reaper says and looks to my dad and brother who are sitting next to my sister. "Quinten, Ben, if you feel up to it, you're welcome to join us. It's a family thing, food and beer. Giselle will already be at the clubhouse, so you'll get to see her again before we take her to a safe house. We just got to finish making the arrangements for it. But it might be best we get her completely out of the state. If we do that, I'm sorry, but to keep her safe, we're not gonna tell you where we're sending her."

I stiffen at Reaper's words, I'm not in the inner circle, but I know there are a few clubs they're allies with and could potentially send her to stay safe with. I'm sure they're all good guys, but they're not the Satan's Keepers. I don't know them, so I don't know if I could trust them. Not like I do those of this club.

"Come on, Butterfingers." Beast guides me away from the group, and I don't get to finish listening to what my brother's and dad's responses are. I feel like my whole world is spinning out of control, and I know if I can hold on or not. It's like I'm losing my grip on what I thought I had control over, and that's not a good feeling for me.

Outside, Beast takes me directly to his bike, swings a leg over it, and climbs on. He doesn't even look at me as he waits for me to follow his direction. The thought of arguing with him crosses my mind, but honestly, I just want to go home, have a glass of wine, and snuggle with Jagger. I want to be left alone.

I'm sure the last thing I want won't happen. Or maybe it will. With the way Beast is acting, I'm sure he just wants to get rid of me, but then, if that were the case, he wouldn't have said what he said to Reaper and the others.

Maybe he has other plans. Those that don't involve me. A part of me dreads the thought. Could he just be taking me back to my house in order to tell me whatever this is going on between us is over? What if he does want us to be over, and he intends to go sleep with someone else?

The very idea of it causes my chest to ache. He's been all I ever wanted and never within reach. Tears burn in my eyes, but I refuse to let them fall. Instead, I climb on the bike behind Beast. I wrap my arms around his middle and hold on. If this is the last ride, I get to have with him, I'm going to savor it all. No one else has ever put me on the back of their bike, and no one else ever will.

The ride home feels far too short for my liking. I want to keep going on forever, but nothing lasts forever. No matter how much you hold on to it or how tightly you grasp it.

Beast parks the bike next to my car in the detached garage, and I climb off the back, somewhat confused by this. The other days of the week, he parked his bike right behind the house. So, him parking in the garage, or even having a remote to it, kind of freaks me out. Especially with the way he's acting.

Or maybe it's the way I'm acting.

I'm not sure.

Needing space, I don't wait for him to join me. I make my way quietly up to the house. Unlocking the back door, I step in, feeling Beast coming up behind me. We're met by Jagger, and I bend down and scoop a meowing Jagger.

"Hey, pretty boy," I murmur and shove my face in his fur while moving through the house, tossing my keys on the table.

Beast keeps quiet, but I can all but feel him as I make my way through the house toward my room, where I plop Jagger on the bed, move to my closet, and toe off the heels I'd worn to work. The whole time, I try to ignore Beast.

Moving to my bathroom, I unbutton my blouse on

the way, removing it and leaving myself in my slacks and cami. I close the door slightly and put my hair up in a knot on the top of my head. I go ahead and clean the makeup from my face, then moisturize. If I don't, my skin will dry out and scream from the lack of moisturizer. It's hard to focus on this with Beast standing in the doorway where it's still open, his eyes boring into me, almost calculating, assessing.

I finish in the bathroom and turn toward Beast, hoping to get past him, but he doesn't budge. Doesn't say a word either.

"Can you move, please?" I ask.

Instead of answering with words or stepping back for me to pass, Beasts steps into my space and encases me in his arms. One hand going up, and the other holding me to him. He sinks his fingers in my hair holding tight while pulling back, forcing me to have to look up. His mouth is there to meet mine, tongue thrusting in my mouth. I grip his shirt and do the only thing I can, I hold on to him.

My knees weaken under me, and if Beast weren't holding me up, I'd collapse. Beast lets go of my hair, some of it falling from the hair tie that was to keep it up. Without letting my mouth go, he slides both hands under the curve of my ass and lifts. I wrap my arms around his neck, and my legs go around his waist.

Beast spins us and carries me the short distance to the bed.

It's only then I realize he'd already stripped off his cut and boots.

Breaking away from the kiss, Beast grips my cami, and takes it up and over my breasts. His gaze stares down at my bare breasts, and a throaty growl of approval fills the room.

I hadn't worn a bra that day, that's what the cami was for. My breasts felt heavy this morning, and I hadn't wanted to put a bra on. Considering I'm a solid C, I'm thankful they're still nice and perky because otherwise, I definitely wouldn't have been able to.

Beast stares at them while he undoes the clasp, holding my pants secure. I hold my breath as he pulls them down my legs, exposing the skimpy sheer black thong I decided to wear.

"Fuck," he growls and jerks them the rest of the way off. He spreads my thighs and settles between them. "I've been wanting to taste this pussy for too damn long." A shiver of excitement rushes through me when he runs his nose along my inner thigh, and one of his fingers rubs against the ultra-thin fabric covering where I want him most.

"Beast," I whisper, my body withering against the sheets, wanting him to do more.

So much more.

Beast draws away, those intense eyes of his boring into mine, holding me captive. "I'm fuckin' you tonight, Bristol. I'm gonna take you every way I've wanted to take you for years now. By the time I finish you, whatever the fuck it is you've had in your head all afternoon and evening, better be a fuckin' thing of the past."

Before I can respond or even let those words sink in fully, Beast's mouth is on my pussy, tongue plunges inside my entrance, and I nearly die of utter embarrassment because there's no stopping myself from coming just from him putting his mouth on me. It's unlike anything I've ever known.

"Fuck, you taste good." Beast groans approvingly. His breath sends tingles of pleasure washing over me.

God, I don't even know if there's any real way of putting it for it to make sense. I've never felt anything like it, though, and I want more.

Beast uses that tongue of his to drive me insane. Not stopping when I initially came so quickly as I thought he might. Instead, he keeps going, adding two fingers while he rotates back and forth between swirling his tongue around my clit and pumping it in my entrance. Doing all this, he draws not just one or two orgasms from me but three. Three blissful, amazing orgasms. I don't think it's possible to take more, yet I do. Beast doesn't stop devouring me until I'm screaming from his ravish hunger.

A whimper leaves my lips, and Beast pulls away. I want him to keep doing what he's doing, but as he rises over me, I definitely want what he's about to give me.

"Gonna fuck you, Butterfingers, nice and slow like." Gripping my ankles, he places them on his shoulders, his cock presses against my entrance.

"What if I don't want nice and slow?" I pant, lifting my bottom, wanting him inside me already. "What if I want fast and hard?"

"Too bad, baby, I'm not about to take you any other way than slow. Your tight pussy wouldn't be able to handle it. You didn't get to lose that virginity of yours the way you should have, and I'm gonna give you the sweet you should have had that first time."

Oh my God. How could he have known that?

"Please, Beast, take me now before I go insane with my need for you to be inside me."

If he doesn't slide his cock in me soon, I'll perish. I ache for him . . . to feel his thick cock inside me, filling me.

"You on the pill, Bristol?" he asks, slipping an inch inside.

"Yes, now fuck me, Beast," His name comes out on a scream as he thrusts home, giving me what I want most of all. "Oh, God, yes, Beast, it feels so good," I cry out, withering around beneath him, wanting more.

Beast growls and dips down, his mouth covering mine. His tongue plunges in my mouth, driving me more insane as his thrusts pick up and he powers inside me, intensifying . . . more like magnifying the sensations washing over me. The rough, gravelly groans that come from his lips as he pulls his lips from mine just heightens the whole experience all the more.

A gasp leaves my parted lips when Beast suddenly moves, rolling us until I'm straddling him from above. "Ride me," he commands. "Ride me until you're coming all over my cock. I want to watch as you come for me."

"Beast," I cry out, doing just as he orders. I ride him, grind my pussy down and rotate my hips. I do this with his hands at my waist, guiding me, showing me exactly what I need to do. His hips buck upward, and I'm unsure of exactly what to do with my hands other than brace them on his chest while I hold myself upright.

My release finds me quickly, and I throw my head back. Beast's name on my lips as I pant and try to see past the stars shattering my vision. It's truly a beautiful thing, yet it scares me at the same time. Beast growls and snarls, his cock jerks inside me, and his release fills me, coating the walls of my pussy. I swear, as he comes, his release washes over my very essence, becoming a part of me.

Falling forward, I collapse on top of Beast, breathing heavily.

"That was . . ." I utter breathlessly.

"Yeah," he finishes for me, not actually finishing, but he knows what I was trying to say. "Fuckin' magnificent."

I definitely have to agree with him, even as that fear threatens to take hold of me once again. However, this feeling is overruled by what Beast said earlier.

The only question now is, do I hold on to what I really want or push him away? Sutton told me months ago to think about what I want, and I never did. I guess now I really need to do just that.

Beast pulls me out of my thoughts by rolling us back over until he's holding himself over me with his elbows keeping his weight from crushing me. "Time for round two, baby," he announces, thrusting inside me.

"Round two?" I stare at him, gaping at the impossibility of such a thing. There's no way he could be ready to go again so soon.

"Yeah, round two. Told you, I was fuckin' you all weekend. I'll let you rest somewhat, but my cock will still be inside you, baby. Like I said earlier. I'm fuckin' you until you can't think of anything else, and I damn well meant it."

I blink at him in astonishment, my lips parting on a breath, and he takes the opportunity to claim my mouth once more.

CHAPTER 10

BEAST

"Fuck yeah, baby, just like that." I tangle my fingers in Bristol's hair as her head bobs up and down on my cock. This, I got to admit, is the best damn way to wake up in the morning.

Bristol seems to love exploring sexual acts, which works for me since I have plenty that we're going to be doing together. I definitely am not going to complain when she enjoys sucking me off. Yesterday, we stayed in bed all day. I fucked her, we slept, fucked some more, and then even more. I took her in every way I've always thought about and more. I didn't know she was so damn flexible, but hell, if I'm not enjoying it.

When I wasn't fucking her in the bed, I took her against the counter in the kitchen, on the couch, and even on the living room floor after we rolled off the couch. Swear I'm addicted to her pussy. And this mouth of hers.

Bristol hums around my shaft, and it goes straight to my balls. I'm ready to blow, and I intend to do it, shooting a load down her throat. Taking control of her movements, I hold her still and thrust up into her mouth, touching the back of her throat. When the first jets of cum spurt from the head, I hold her still while spraying it all down her throat. With the last spasms leaving my cock, I let Bristol's hair go and drop back against the headboard with a groan.

"Damn, that mouth of yours." I let out a breath and watch as she lifts her mouth off my cock, her tongue peeking out to lick the crest. Needing to be inside her, I reach for her and drag her up and over me. "Sit on my dick, baby. I want that tight pussy wrapped around me."

"Mhmm," she hums and does as I tell her.

I let her ride me for a while, but when she finishes, I intend to be the one to make that happen. Feeling her walls tighten and spasm, I flip her to her back, lift her legs over my shoulders, and fuck her hard. Bristol's screams of pleasure are music to my ears.

Sweat beads my forehead, dripping down between her perky tits. Those beauties are another thing I've spent time enjoying. Tasting her all over has been nothing if not delectable.

I draw two more releases from her before I succumb to my own, groaning as her pussy clamps down on me, sucking me dry.

"Damn, I'm addicted to your sweet pussy, baby." I groan, leaning down to kiss her. "Wish I'd taken the time to eat you before fuckin' you, but I'll just have to do that later on."

"I'll make sure to hold you to that," she whispers, trying to catch her breath still. "I need to get a shower."

"Yeah," I agree. "We gotta get to the clubhouse soon. It's already after noon, and we're gonna be late for the cookout."

"Do we have to go?" Bristol asks. A moan passes her lips as I pull out of her slick heat. "Couldn't we stay here? I mean, as much as I've enjoyed what we've been doing, I still have some things I need to get done. Like laundry and spend time with Jagger."

"We can do that all when we get back. I promise we won't be there all day, but we're going, Butterfingers. You're gonna want to see your sister before she leaves tomorrow." Bristol nods, but I can see her mind starting to spin, and I'm going to have to put a stop to it. "Don't, Bristol," I grunt. "You're not going to start overthinking shit. You got something [to] talk to me."

"Why are you doing all this? Why [take my] dad's call? You didn't want to be a pa[rt of it] and yet you allowed him to bring you into our family problems." Bristol climbs out of bed, grabs my shirt off the floor, and pulls it over her head. "For that matter, why after all this time, are you doing any of this? You never wanted me before?"

"I've always wanted you," I growl, getting out of bed. I snag my jeans off the floor and yank them on, leaving them unbuttoned. I close the distance between us, gripping her waist with one hand, and her chin with the other. "Don't even doubt that I didn't."

"Yeah, you wanted me, but you refused to do anything about it," she scoffs.

"Because you were an employee," I retort, but even I know that's a lie. One I've been telling myself for years. I refused to do anything about it because I didn't want her to get hurt by the world that I came from. My family isn't normal. Yeah, they're wealthy, but that wealth comes with a curse. I didn't want my past to affect Bristol. Even now the very thought of it scares the shit out of me, however, I'm not about to give her up. I can't and won't.

I left months ago in order to get her out of my head, but it didn't happen. She's burrowed deep in my skin, there's no getting her out. I've decided I want to keep her there, and that means not letting her go.

"Whatever." Bristol rolls her eyes and tries to step away, but I don't let her.

"It's not fuckin' whatever, Bristol, and you damn well know it." Dropping my grip on her chin, I wrap both arms around her waist and draw her flush against my front. "But you're right, that wouldn't have kept me from getting in your pants, but I knew even then that you mean something to me, and I wasn't goin' to fuck that up. You in my life was too damn important, and I wasn't going to let you get hurt because of my past."

"And yet you got drawn into my family drama," she bites out, narrowing her eyes to little slits.

"Yeah, I did, but I don't give a fuck. Your sister needed help. The club's doing that for her because they know, on some level, she means something to you, and you mean something to all of us. I could have easily told your dad to fuck off, but I didn't because the other night you told me he wasn't like your mom, and I saw that for myself the other day. So damn right, I got involved." I want to be pissed with her, but I can't. This was the conversation we needed to have Friday night, but we ended up going straight to fucking.

"I don't get you." A look of confusion crosses Bristol's gaze, and I don't blame her.

"Look, let's get through the day at the clubhouse with the cookout, and tonight, I'll explain things so they're a bit clearer."

Bristol's eyes bore into mine, darting over my face, taking in the sincerity of my words or looking for any sort of deception. Finally, she lets out a breath and nods. "Fine, but you better have a good explanation."

I grin and kiss her softly. "I promise tonight, we'll talk, and I'll give you my reasons for everything."

CHAPTER 11

BRISTOL

"Hop off, Butterfingers," Beast says, patting my thigh.

"Okay." I sigh and let go of his waist, sliding my fingers up to grip his shoulders. I hold on to him to balance myself while climbing off the back of his bike.

No sooner did I get both feet on the ground, I hear Paxton and Sage shouting and running in my direction.

"Auntie Brissy," Sage squeals. I squat down, arms out, ready for her hug, but nothing can prepare me for both kids to plow right into me, wrapping their arms around my neck and sending me to my bottom. If Beast wasn't directly behind me, they'd take me the rest of the way to my back. "We mistied you," Sage announces, stepping back alongside her brother while Beast helps me from the ground.

"I've missed you guys too." I smile, reach out, and run my fingers through the little girl's curly locks. "I'll talk to your mom about next weekend, getting you two and having a sleepover at my house. How's that sound?"

"Fuckin' fantastic," Reaper calls out, coming up to scoop Sage in his arms and looking down at Paxton. "Come on, little man, your mom has your plates ready for you."

"Yay! Hot dogs are the shish," Paxton yells, pumping his fist.

"Reaper, seriously." I giggle, unable to help myself. "Ivy is going to kill you."

"No, she won't." Reaper grins and walks off.

"Oh yeah, she will," I shout, speaking to his back.

Beast wraps an arm around my shoulders, chuckling. "Come on, baby, let's get over there. I see your dad and brother watching us."

My steps falter, and I glance around, finding both men standing there in jeans. Jeans. I don't think I've ever seen either of them wear jeans in my life. Well, maybe Ben, but never my dad. Those jeans were even paired with T-shirts, not polos or dress shirts. They look totally normal and definitely not out of place. Sitting down at the table next to them is my sister, and she still looks the same because of the bruises, but she's wearing a T-shirt dress. I'm sure it's loose on her for reasons I already know.

"Bristol?" Beast gives my shoulder a squeeze and urges me forward.

"This is all too weird," I mumble, more to myself.

"It'll be okay," Beast murmurs and kisses the side of my head. "Just don't think too hard on it."

"Easy for you to say." I was still freaked out. The two of us spent a lot of time having sex since that first time and didn't really stop until we passed out, even when Beast's cock was inside me. I loved every memorable moment of the sex-a-thon. He'd been right about me not thinking of anything else. I didn't until after he mentioned going to the clubhouse. His telling me that he would explain things to me later definitely freaks me out, although I'll admit to myself it also excites me because I'll be learning more about who he is.

Beast drops his hand from around my shoulder, and I feel a knot in the pit of my stomach, thinking it was going to draw away from me, but he surprises me by taking my hand in his. He surprises me even more by lifting my hand upward to press a kiss to my palm.

"Bristol," my dad greets me when we're in close range and pulls me in for a hug.

"Hey, Dad." I smile and return his hug before stepping back and smiling at Ben and then my sister. "I hope you all are having a good time."

"It's definitely a new experience," Giselle murmurs, looking around. "Last night I heard more sexual sounds than I've ever heard before." She gives me a shy look while I notice her blushing.

"Yeah, these guys get kind of rowdy." I laugh nervously.

"Glad you guys could make it," Beast says, pulling me back into his arms and chuckling. "Have y'all ate anything yet?"

"We were waiting on Bristol," Ben answers.

"Figured we could all eat together," my dad says, smiling, glancing between the two of us, his eyes holding a look of approval in them.

"Why don't you sit here with your sister, and I'll grab you a plate," Beast offers.

I give him a nod as my answer and make my way around to the opposite side of the picnic table and take a seat. From where I'm sitting, I can see Beast as he, my dad, and my brother all start toward the table filled with food. I catch Ivy's gaze and wave at her. Sutton turns and she waves. Isabelle sees me, disconnects from the others, and starts in our direction along with Stella and Everleigh. I see Josephine sitting at another table holding her newborn baby boy.

"You have an amazing life with these people," Giselle remarks, drawing my attention to her. "I'm happy you were able to find happiness."

"Thanks, Elle." I smile. "They are all great people."

"I can see that." There's a look of envy in my sister's eyes.

"You have some explaining to do, woman," Isabelle declares, planting her bottom next to me on the bench. Usually, she's super shy and doesn't talk to anyone unless she knows you well. I've come to know her well, and I can see the gleam in her eyes. "Spill it, I know you and Beast finally had sex. After what happened, are you okay?"

I can't help but wince, knowing she's talking about Potter. I want to change the subject, especially since Giselle is right here, but considering what she's been through, she'll probably understand.

I chance a quick glance at her, then look to where Beast is still getting food on plates while talking to his brothers. Finally, I return my attention to Isabelle. "I'm okay. I didn't even think about what happened to me. Or the scars." That last part is not more than a breath.

"What happened to you?" Giselle asks, looking between Isabelle and me.

Taking a deep breath, I answer, "I was kidnapped, raped, and nearly killed by a psycho."

Giselle's eyes widen and she looks taken back. "How in the world didn't we know this?"

"Because the club kept it quiet." Thankfully, it was Isabelle who answered for me. "Reaper and the others knew it would be the best way to protect her at the time."

"I'm so sorry," Giselle whispers, and I can't help but flinch because that's the last thing I want to hear. No one ever wants to hear anyone saying those words out of pity. "I wish I knew what you'd been through. Maybe I could have come to you sooner." I whip my gaze back to hers on that last bit and stare at my sister in utter disbelief as she inhales, tears glistening in her eyes. "Ronnie's always hit me from the moment we got back from the honeymoon. But over the two years we were married, it got worse. This last year he's raped me more than once."

"What made you finally ask for help?" I blurt the question and want to kick myself for asking it.

"I'm pregnant," she admits. "I could deal with it myself, the beatings, even the rape, but I didn't want to put a child through that."

Whoa.

I swallow past the lump forming in my throat and look from Giselle to Isabelle and then back to my sister. I can respect the fact she's finally decided to leave in order to protect her child.

"Did Ronnie know you were pregnant before you left?" That's something we all need to know, and I hope he doesn't because if he did, there's no way he'll let her go. Not without a fight.

"I found out after he left for work," Giselle says, licking her busted lip once again. "I knew if he found out, it would enrage him. He has a plan for when we're to have children, and he'd beat me worse than he did Thursday night after getting back from the poker game. He'd lost and came home to take it out on me."

Tears prick my eyes, and it's all I can do to keep from letting them spill down my cheeks. I want to cry for my sister and what she's been going through. I wish I'd known exactly what she was going through. I'd have sent someone after her a long time ago.

"Does anyone else know you're pregnant?" I ask.

"Stella and the rest of us know she's pregnant," Isabelle answers, reaching across the table to take my sister's hand in hers. "We told her we'd be here for her."

So that's why Isabelle came over here. To give my sister support as well as me. To make it easier for the both of us to understand each other.

I open my mouth to say something else but close it when Beast, my dad, and my brother all sit back down. I won't say anything in front of any of them. Not unless she speaks up first. I don't know if I'll be able to keep from saying anything to Beast when we're alone, though. With my sister pregnant, I don't know if sending her away will be for the best. She'll be alone, where here, she has family close by.

Either way, my sister's pregnant, and shouldn't be alone to take care of this child without someone to help her.

"What's going through your head, Butterfingers?" Beasts asks me a couple of hours later.

The afternoon ended up being a good one. My family seemed to have a good time and were really laid back. I realized while eating that it was definitely always my mother who made things so tense. None of them were involved in the tension. Well, that is unless you count them being tense because of her. We were never able to be an actual family, and for the first time today, we got to do that, and it was great.

I brush a strand of my hair out of my face and meet Beast's gaze. Honestly, I'm not sure what I'm seeing. He looks curious, yet concerned, but there's something else, and I just can't put my finger on it. "Why do you ask?"

Beast pulls me close, his larger body molding against mine as we sit on one of the benches. With all the children having gone either home or to their parents' rooms to sleep, the skanks have come out of hiding. My dad and brother left, and my sister went back to her room. Beast and I have been enjoying the party. Some of his brothers had come over and talked with us, including me in the conversation. It feels good that they do this even if I don't know what they're talking about.

Now, it's just the two of us sitting alone with a bonfire going not too far away. Only the glow of the flames lights up the night air.

"I can see it in your eyes, Bristol," Beast murmurs, leaning in, he rubs his nose against mine. "Something's been on your mind all day. Now, it's time to talk to me."

Sighing, I look away as I tell him. "My sister's pregnant. That's why she finally left Ronnie."

"Fuck. Did he know she was pregnant?"

I knew this would be asked.

"She said he didn't know, but you know men like him don't let go without a fight. If he finds out, she's in more trouble than ever. But also, if she goes anywhere, she's without family to help her with this baby."

"You don't want to lose your sister," Beast announces, stating it more to himself.

"Yes," I whisper.

"I'll talk to Reaper and the others in the morning during church. See what we can do so you don't have to lose her 'cause you're right, she'd be without family, and after what she's been through, she's gonna need us."

"Us?" I jerk back and stare at him in confusion.

"Yeah, us, baby. Your dad and brother, you and me. She'll need all of us to get through this."

My heart leaps in my chest, and I want to believe him. I really do, but I'm so confused. "We still need to have that talk, Beast." I find myself saying.

"And we're gonna have that as soon as we get back to the house," Beast declares and gets to his feet, bringing me with him. "Time to go home."

Holding my hand, Beast guides me to his bike, gets on, and waits for me to join him.

Fifteen minutes later, we pull into my driveway only to find two vehicles there, neither of them I recognize, alongside a cop's car.

"What the hell?" I murmur to myself because I know there's no way Beast could have heard me.

Beast parks the bike and no sooner he turns the key for it, my mother is there.

"Where have you been?" she demands.

"What are you doing here?" I snap and look past her to see not only an officer but Ronnie and Cordell standing off to the side. Both men glaring in our direction.

"I asked you first." My mom reaches for me. "And get off that death trap. You're embarrassing me by being on the back of some biker's motorcycle like some whore."

"I suggest you back away, lady," Beast advises, climbing off the back of his bike and taking me with him. Our movements are flawless as he maneuvers us like so. When he positions himself in front of me, he speaks directly to the officer. "Bryant, want to explain what you all are doing here at my woman's house?"

"Your woman?" Officer Bryant cocks a brow. "I was told this was Cordell Barker's fiancée's home."

"You would be mistaken," Beast grunts and squeezes my hand. "Bristol isn't Cordell's fiancée, she's mine."

Oh my God. He did not just say that.

"Excuse me. That is a lie." Mom seethes.

"Not a lie, lady. Her father gave me his blessing and all. I can call him right now if you'd like and let him tell you himself." Beast surprises me, though it honestly shouldn't. Beast knows what he's doing, and I trust him.

"That bastard. He has no right to give any blessings after what he's done." I watch as my mother's expression contorts, and she steps forward.

Officer Bryant steps in front of her. "Ma'am, I'll ask you to calm down and step back so we can get this matter sorted."

"There's nothing to settle here, Bryant," Beast remarks.

"You might think that, but there's more to discuss,

such as Bristol's missing sister. Do either of you know where she might be?"

I bite my tongue to keep from speaking out and let Beast handle this.

"We haven't seen or heard from Bristol's sister since Monday last week when she and their mother came here to cause a scene as her mother is doing now," Beast answers, his voice calm and cool, but I felt the tension in his body. "Bristol doesn't have much of a relationship with any of her family, and they all are aware of this, so why would her sister be in contact?"

"Right." Officer Bryant grunts, nodding. "If you do see or hear from Giselle, think you can let these folks know?"

"Not my business or my woman's," I remark, making it known to Byrant that I sure as hell wouldn't be telling them shit without saying it outright. I know the game and I'm not about to give them an inclination into what they want.

"Officer, I'm sorry, but even if I did, I wouldn't call any of these people," I mutter, unable to help myself. Stepping fully around Beast but staying where he can wrap an arm around my waist and pull me into his side, I point a finger in my mother's direction while speaking further to the police officer.

"For one, I don't have a relationship with this woman. No matter what she says or does. Nor do I have anything to do with either of those other two men. I'm not Cordell Barker's fiancée or anything to him. As for Ronnie, considering he's nothing but a piece of shit who thinks his ass smells like a bed of roses, I wouldn't be surprised if my sister packed up and took off to Aruba or somewhere far away from here just to get away from him. For the record, regardless of a bed of roses or not, an ass still smells like an ass."

Beast snorts, and Officer Bryant laughs outright.

"Well then, I'll let you two get on with your night and get these three off your property." Officer Bryant grins and shakes his head. "But if you do hear from your sister, please contact me," he says, reaching into his pocket and pulling out a card. "You can reach me on either number on there."

"Will do." I take the card, wave it, and shove it in my pocket. "Now, if you'll excuse me," I remark, curling deeper into Beast's side. "My fiancé and I were heading inside to go to bed, if you know what I mean." I make sure to meet my mother's glare as I say this last part before Beast guides me away from the group of people in the driveway. He draws a key out of his pocket and unlocks the door. I hadn't even known he had a key until just now, and I should ask him about it, but I have other things to worry about right now. All of them are more important than a measly key.

Inside, I reach down and unzip my boots from my feet and take them off while Jagger comes to greet me. Barefoot, I scoop my cat in my arms and turn to face Beast as he empties his pockets.

"We're going to have to warn Giselle," I whisper.

"I'll talk to my brothers tomorrow during church about what just went down." He grunts, looks at the cat in my arms, and shakes his head. "Can't fuck you if you're holding the cat, Butterfingers."

"Well, I guess it's a good thing we're not going to be going to bed. We still have things to discuss. You promised."

"Yeah, I did." Beast grunts and makes his way through the house to the kitchen, where he opens the refrigerator, snagging one of the beers he bought and put in there. He then pours me a glass of wine. "Sit down, baby."

Silently, I curl into the corner of my couch and accept the glass from him as he joins me. Jagger meows and leaves me to sit in Beast's lap. The little traitor that he is.

Beast drinks half his beer before he finally sets it down and meets my gaze as he starts talking. "You know who my brother is and that I come from a family much similar to yours. Growing up, it was fine living there. That is until I found out a few things I didn't want to know." The way he shakes his head and lets out a breath has my gut tightening. "My mother's side of the family is from royalty."

"What?" I breathe, eyes widening in surprise.

"I don't want to get into it and how that all is, but my grandmother turned her back on her family, and married my grandfather. He was killed just a couple years later after my mother was born. Out of fear, my grandmother made a deal with them that if they left her alone, then she'd ensure her firstborn grandson would be theirs so long as they left her and her daughter alone."

"Oh my God." I can't believe what I'm hearing.

"Anyway, my mother and father married, and I'm the firstborn. My grandmother kept this all a secret until after my first birthday. My mother's cousin evidently came to collect me, and that caused problems within the family. My father and grandfather, they weren't about to give me over to anyone. My mother refused to let me go. She'd been devastated, so much so she refused to speak to her mother, and because of this, my grandmother killed herself.

Beast reaches for his beer, finishes off the last of it, and sets the bottle back down with a thud. "Fast forward to when I was sixteen. I walked in on my father and mother talking about me supposedly marrying someone. I wasn't about that and demanded to know. That's when they told me about all of this.

Not happy, I took off for a year, refusing to talk to them or anyone else. I lived on the streets and learned to handle myself. It's how I met Diablo. We had each other's backs."

"One night, I decided to just go home. I missed my family. That's when I walked in on my mother being tagged teamed by both my grandfather and father. Not something anyone wants to see. Evidently, it was part of the deal they all made. Both father and son would share my mother. It made me sick to my stomach, and I walked away. A week later, my father found me, and the two of us went to a bar where he explained things even more to me. According to him, it's what my mother wanted. She was in love with both men, and to free me, she had to have another kid. Not Everett, he was already born, but she had to give over a child to her cousin or face death."

"How could her family do that?" I gasp. "Or yours, for that matter?"

"I don't know. I didn't ask. It was fucked up, in my opinion, and I didn't want him to tell me anymore. I don't know if she had the kid or not. I told my father I didn't want anything to do with him or anyone else in the family. But to make matters worse, the old man had to tell me a few things about his side of the family. Said it's the way of the world they walk in. See, my aunt, Cordell's mother, her marriage was a business arrangement, and according to my father, to the outside world, she's a beautiful woman from society, but in reality, she's nothing more than a slave to her husband. She's to do everything he says without so much as speaking."

"To get away from all of this, I refuse to speak to any of them. I want nothing to do with them and cut all contact with them. My father's only request was to always have a number to be able to reach me in case of an emergency. I allowed this, and he's never contacted me. He hadn't used that number until he gave it to your dad."

My mind is whirling with all the information he's just dropped on me, and I cock my head slightly. "So, you were on your own at seventeen?"

"More like sixteen. I might have gone back, but once I saw what I did, I left again and never returned. I preferred to leave on the streets," he grunts. "But not long after that, Diablo and I found ourselves taken in by the Satan's Keepers MC. It's where we belong."

"How did you get your road name?" Something had to happen to get it. No one gets a road name without something happening.

"The night the Satan's Keepers MC took us in, I killed three men with my bare hands. They were enemies of the club and had just attacked one of the brothers outside of one of the establishments they were running out of at the time. Diablo and the club member said I was like a beast on a rampage. Afterward, Diablo set fire to the three men and covered any evidence that could possibly lead back to me. After that, we took the brother back to the clubhouse as he asked us to, and Reaper took us in. He just became President. We've been with the club ever since," he says, watching me closely.

I sit silently, letting the weight of all that he shares sink in. Not just about his family but how he got his name. That's something I never expected, but it also shows how much faith he puts in me. Setting my still-full wine glass on the coffee table, I crawl the small distance between the two of us and settle in his lap with my fingers wrapping around his neck.

I stare into those beautiful dark eyes of his and lean in, pressing my forehead against his for a moment before I press my lips to his. Words aren't going to be able to do anything in this moment. Right now, the best thing I can give him to show him my appreciation and that I'm not scared is to give him my trust. He may have already had my body, but not like this. Tonight, it's not going to be hard and fast or just about the sex. It's about connecting. The two of us finally getting on the same page and knowing what we have is real. We're both cut from the same cloth in some ways. It's why we fit so well together and make sense.

But I do think that he and his brother should talk and reconnect. That relationship was severed when it shouldn't have been. And to hold on to him, to get him over what's happened in the past, I'll start with getting them close again.

CHAPTER 12

BEAST

"I'll pick you up after work today," I inform Bristol the moment we step onto the floor of her office building, and I have her at her desk. As much as I want to get out of here before seeing my little brother, I'm going to have to talk to him. Tell him if Ronnie or Cordell come by here, I need to know, and more importantly, if her mother stops by. I'm not going to leave her unprotected.

I'm sure Everett is competent enough to look out for Bristol. I had Scythe look into him and find out he's not just some hotshot, but he's a fucking cutthroat in the business. I shouldn't be surprised. He was always a fighter and sharp-minded when we were kids.

Fuck.

In the past week, I've thought more of my family, more or less of Everett, than I have in the past. It makes me question whether or not my mom ever did have another kid. Growing up, I loved my parents and cherished my mother. That was until the blinders were ripped right off, and I saw them for who they really were.

"Okay," Bristol says and moves around her U-shaped desk, eyes scanning over everything scattered around. "Everett must have worked this weekend. Swear I don't know how he does his job with how disorganized he leaves things. He could have put everything back where they belong."

I can't help but smirk as she goes on grumbling and fixes the folders and papers on her desk. "You know when he's going to be in?" Just as the question leaves my mouth, Everett's office door opens.

"Never left," Everett says, brushing a hand through his hair, eyes on me. "I'm surprised you're still here." He jerks his chin up and cocks a brow, that smug expression in place.

"Need to talk to you," I inform him and start in his direction but halt my steps as Bristol snaps.

"About what? Everett has work to do, and you have to get to the clubhouse."

I cock my head in her direction and stare at her.

What the hell is she getting pissed about? "Gotta talk to him before I go, baby."

"You don't have time," she declares, planting her hands on her hips, her eyes narrowing. "If it has anything to do with what I'm thinking, you can do your talking right here in front of me."

Crossing my arms, I give her my full attention. "And if it's something I need to speak privately with my brother?"

"Unless it's something you really think I don't need to hear, more than what you told me last night, then you don't have anything to hide, right?"

Fuck me. Does she have to be sexy while trying to go head-to-head with me? My cock throbs, and I'm not against fucking her right here on her desk, but I'm not going to do it in front of my brother. I'm not like my father and able to do something like that, not with the woman I claim as mine. Even with the PPs at the clubhouse, I'd take them in the shadows, never with anyone watching.

"What's going on here?" Everett demands, his tone going fully alert.

"You have court today, you take her with you. If she's working, she sticks with you, going where you go. No leaving her here at the office alone."

"Beast, the office has security, nothing is going to happen." Bristol huffs.

"Don't give a fuck. They're not going to stop your mother, Ronnie, and Cordell from getting to you here if they want to attempt it." Those names leave a bad taste in my mouth and the need for blood, their blood, would be preferable.

"Cordell?" Everett spits out. "As in Cordell Barker?"

"The one and same." I nod.

"What the fuck is going on that involves him?" Everett steps closer, eyes darting between the two of us. "What has he done now?"

"Not just him, Everett," I grunt. "His buddy, Ronnie, is married to Bristol's sister Giselle and is an abuser. She left him. Cordell seems to think Bristol is his fiancée, and Bristol's mother is a bitch from hell who wants my woman's trust fund."

"I knew about the last part," Everett remarks glumly, meeting my gaze. "Dad informed me of this, this weekend while I spoke to him on the phone." Something in his eyes flashes, and I want to question it, but I shove the need back.

"Wait, you knew who my family was?" Bristol asks, staring gapingly at my little brother.

"Of course, I did," Everett scoffs. "I knew. I wouldn't be who I am today if I didn't know who I surrounded myself with. I knew taking you on as my assistant would lead me back to my big brother." My little brother cocks his head, rolling it side to side. "I'm no idiot. I learned a long time ago to handle myself." His gaze shifts and locks solely on me. "You and I, big brother, have a lot to discuss, and since I'm sensing Bristol knows . . ."

"She knows about our family. At least my part in the family," I grunt, jaw tight, my back teeth clenched.

"Right, then you can both hear the rest of it," Everett advises. "Our mother died in childbirth, the child with her."

My chest aches for the mother I used to know, but I don't let them know his words affect me.

"Dad and Granddad kept the information minimal to the public as they didn't want it getting out to Mom's side. They're protecting the both of us with this information because the Swedish cousins aren't happy to have been denied what they want."

"Swedish?" Bristol mutters, looking at me.

"Yeah," I grumble. "They're royal but no claim to the throne."

"Then why are they so hell-bent on all of this?" I can see the demand in her gaze, along with the confusion.

"Because they're vindictive assholes who are fucked in the head," Everett mutters. "But more than that, they're evil and demand blood when crossed, meaning they'll come for you."

That's what I didn't want to hear.

It also answers my question on why my dad gave Quinten the number he has for me. He could have told Quinten he didn't know and easily sent him through other channels. That was him giving me the silent message that trouble could be coming my way.

I denied my family, but that doesn't change the fact those on my mother's side want what they were promised. This means that by claiming Bristol, she'll be in even more danger than I thought she was with what's going on with her family.

My phone beeps in my pocket, and I pull it out to find a text from Reaper asking where I'm at. I quickly shoot him a message back, saying I'll be there soon. Shoving the damn thing back in my pocket, I look at my brother.

"With that damn shit to think about, I'm gonna need to talk to my brothers about this shit. Keep her close to you today. If Cordell or either of those other two come here, you call me." I don't want to leave my woman here without me, but I've got to get to the clubhouse, and I know she's not going to leave when she loves her job. Even if I don't like it, I can see she enjoys what she does working for Everett.

"I'll keep her close," Everett grunts, jerking his chin up. "We've got work to handle anyway." Spinning to my woman in a dismissive manner, he speaks directly to her. "Court was postponed this morning. Instead, we've got the Markers coming along with the Winstons. They want to discuss some issues they're having regarding—"

"I thought they were fighting against each other," Bristol interrupts him.

"Well, I'll let you two get to it," I mutter, moving into Bristol's space. I wrap an arm around her and hold her close. "You need me, call. Otherwise, I'll be back later to pick you up." I kiss her hard and deep before letting her go, leaving her in my brother's hands until I return.

Right now, though, it's time to get to the clubhouse and fill my brothers in on all the shit I've learned. After that, I've got to figure out what the hell we're all gonna do because there's no way I can let my woman's sister go away to a safe house when she's pregnant. I can't leave her without protection because of fucking Cordell and Ronnie, more so because of that mother of hers. Then, to top it off, I've found out that my mother had died, and I didn't even know it. With her, the kid she promised.

God only knows what the Swedish cousins will try to do when they find me. More or less, find Bristol with me. The deal my grandmother made is one with the devil and signed in blood.

Stepping into the clubhouse, the door slams closed behind me. The ride from dropping Bristol off didn't ease the irritation or anger building inside me. Out of the corner of my eye, I spot Giselle sitting with Ivy and Stella. Ivy must not be going into the shop to work today. She and Isabella run that office together, but lately, it's been Isabella, from what I've heard since I got back. According to Diablo, she's been sticking close to home with the twins. I get it, and there's nothing wrong with it. Stella, being a doctor, either has the day off or is going in later.

I don't bother going to greet any of them. I need to get to church and figure this shit out. Too much is swirling around in my head. I've got to be able to protect Bristol if I want to claim her as mine.

Fuck, what am I thinking? That woman is mine, and I damn well know it. Regardless of the demons eating at me. Or my past that seems to be coming. I'll have to fill my brothers in on all the shit they don't know, and I'm not sure how the hell it's going to go. Only a few know I come from money. I don't talk about it, and no one asks. What I tell them might piss a few of my brothers off, but who the fuck knows. Then again, with Everett showing up at the garage the other day, they all already know he's my little brother.

I step over the threshold to find almost everyone already seated. Only Styxx and Scythe are still missing.

"Glad you could make it," Reaper grunts, watching me.

"Had to drop Bristol off at work and talk to Everett, make sure he didn't leave her there unprotected," I grumble, taking my seat by Diablo. The two of us might only be members and not hold rank within the club, but like a few others, we have a place at the table. I never understood it, but I respect Reaper and Angel. They run this club and do a hell of a job doing it as well. All of my brothers and I agree that those two men all but bleed for this club. They've more than earned their ranks, and taking me in the way they did, I appreciate them all the more.

"I thought that building is secure?" Angel remarks in question.

"Yeah, but it won't stop Giselle's husband, Cordell Barker, or that fuckin' mother of Bristol's from getting to her. I wouldn't put it past any of them," I grumble and lean back in my seat, letting out a frustrated breath. "The three of them decided to pay Bristol a visit last night. They were at the house when we got there along with Officer Bryant."

"I bet Bryant enjoyed that visit," Tombstone scoffs as both Scythe and Styxx step into the room, closing the door behind them.

I'm not surprised to find Scythe has his and Josephine's baby, August, curled up against his chest.

"You couldn't get him to sleep anywhere else?" Reaper smirks.

"Fuck no, tried, and he wouldn't lay down for shit," Scythe grunts, taking his seat. "Josephine needed to get some rest. August woke up every hour last night wanting to eat. Neither of us got shit worth of sleep last night. Doesn't help that the only place the boy wants to sleep is on either of our chests. Though he prefers my woman's tits."

"Don't mind him. He's just irritable 'cause he's got to share Josie's tits with Auggie here." Styxx snorts.

"Kiss my ass." Scythe sneers.

"Fucker, we're twins, shared the same womb. I figure at some point or other, I did that already." Styxx outright laughs.

"Alright, before the two of you can get back into it, we've got shit to deal with right now that doesn't involve ass kissing or tits," Reaper states sternly, putting a stop to all other antics. "Beast, finish filling us in on what happened last night."

I fill them in with all the details of last night, including what Bristol said along with her mother. "I'm not sure what Cordell is playing at, but you should all know if you don't already, the fucker's my cousin, and he's a complete asshole with a vindictive streak a mile long. The mother, though, you all already know what she's attempting. But more than that, Ronnie is going to be after Bristol's sister. He's not going to give up on getting her back, especially if he finds out she's knocked up."

"Fuck, that complicates things," Angel mutters, shaking his head.

"Yeah, that was my thought as well," I agree. "Bristol doesn't want her sister to go away and not have help from her family."

"Then we go need to figure something else out. Bristol is family, and she's never asked for anything. After what she went through, I think we need to make it happen, so she doesn't lose her sister. Any objections?" Reaper grunts, glancing around the table.

Silence is all that meets his question, and he nods.

"What if you talk to Everett? He's a lawyer, not fully connected to us, just through you. What if you get him to do a restraining order?" Diablo suggests.

"You want me to bring my brother into this?" I stare at him in disbelief. He's got to be insane.

"It would be a good option considering if we were to keep her here, she's safe, and they wouldn't be the wiser. If he petitions the court for the order, they wouldn't ask questions, considering the fact he's doing it for his assistant as a favor. Not for the club. We can protect her here."

I stare silently at him, and I get where he's coming from. But there's also the other bullseye that comes with bringing Everett into the fold on this. Taking a deep breath, I roll my head on my shoulders and look directly at Reaper. "There's more that needs to be said. You and Angel know my past, along with a few others . . ." I take the next twenty minutes to fill them all in on the rest of what I need to regarding my mother's family, including her death and that of the child. I still can't believe she was going to give over a child to them, but then again, I can. The mother I thought she was died a long time ago when I first learned all this shit at sixteen. "So, not only do we have to deal with this shit, but I've also got the target that was painted on my back a long time ago now possibly positioned on Bristol's, and I won't lose her."

"You're not going to lose her, Beast," Tombstone remarks sternly.

"Scythe, I want you and Styxx to get to work at the computers and see what you can find on Beast's family. We'll deal with that further once we have it. For now, Beast, call Bristol and get her and Everett in here. Let's talk to him. Diablo's right, having him handle Giselle's restraining order and eventually the custody of the baby, will be a good approach to this. He's not tied to the club, and we all know that he's cutthroat in the courtroom."

"Maybe we should talk to him about taking us on as clients." Hellhound snorts.

"It's a possibility. Now, let's break for the time being, but no one leaves the clubhouse. I want to have a plan in place for Giselle by tonight," Reaper declares, dismissing us all for the time being.

I don't want to think about this all being a good idea where Everett's concerned, but they're right, and I'm just going to have to get over it. I'm going to have to deal with a lot of shit now that my past is coming to the present, and I need to do that before it has the chance to bite me on the ass.

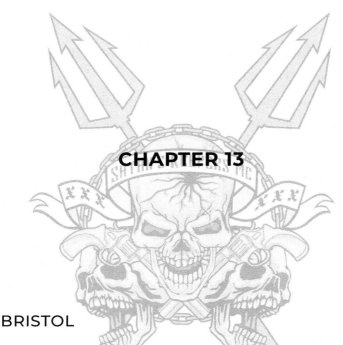

CHAPTER 13

BRISTOL

"Yeah, we're on the way." I glance up at the clipped tone of Everett's voice as he comes through the open doorway to his office to where my desk is set up. "We'll be there in ten, fifteen minutes tops," he states, pulling the phone away from his ear, eyes on me. "Let's go."

"Where are we going?" I ask, already moving, grabbing my purse and phone. "Who was that?"

"My big brother needs us at the clubhouse. We've got to roll," Everett answers, granting me a quick glance and continuing on the way to the elevator.

"Does this have anything to do with what happened yesterday?" I join him, my nerves pricking.

"Don't know all the details yet, babe, but he told me

I needed to get my ass there and bring you with me. Whatever it is, it's important 'cause that fucker hasn't once called my cell. I didn't even know he had the number." We step into the elevator, and I can hear the terseness in his voice. Though I'm not sure, I think there's a bit of something else there. I just don't know what that something is.

I don't speak again because I don't know what else to say. I mean, what do you say to that? Beast hasn't spoken to his brother in years, and then Everett showed up at the garage to drop me off. Then, this morning, Beast stayed to talk to him in order to make sure I'm safe. Now, the Beast is calling his brother's cell. Yeah, I suppose it would bother me a bit. But I want both men to reconnect and have the bond brothers should have.

Beast has already done so much for me, and I realize that now, I want to do the same for him.

The bell of the elevator draws me out of my thoughts, and I step out on the first floor only to come to an abrupt stop. Standing there is none other than my mother with both men, yet again.

"Cordell," Everett grumbles in greeting, stepping in front of me. "To what do I owe the pleasure of your visit?"

Out of the corner of my eye, I notice security is already making their way toward us. Those men were personally hired by Everett. He owns the whole building. Well, his family does. How these three got as far as they did surprises me.

"You need to come with us, Bristol," my mother snaps. "Right now."

"I don't think so." Everett motions to the men approaching. "Trace, please have my cousin and these other two removed from the property."

"Sure thing, boss," Trace states and jerks a chin toward his team.

"You don't want to get involved in this," Cordell warns. "Bristol needs to come with us, or things will get ugly, if you know what I mean."

My breath catches in my throat at the threat Cordell's voice holds.

Maybe I should go with them to stop all of this from happening.

"Go ahead and give it your all, Cordell." Everett chuckles darkly. "Now, if you'll all excuse us, my assistant and I have an appointment to attend to."

Positioning himself, blocking the three pains in the ass from getting close to me, he guides me away from them and out to his car. Everett opens the door for me like the perfect gentleman, but I can feel the tension rolling off him. The moment the door closes me in, he darts around the hood and gets in behind the wheel, wasting no time in shoving the key in the ignition. He pulls away from the curb with a squeal of tires.

"Beast is going to be pissed, but we're going to have to take longer to get there to make sure we're not followed," Everett mutters.

"He'll understand," I say, trying not to let what just happened affect me, no matter how much it actually does. "That is after we tell him what happened with Trouble one, two, and three showing up. Granted, it wasn't really anything."

"It was something," Everett huffs, clenching the steering wheel tightly. "Cordell wasn't playing around. If he wants things to get ugly, he only has to make a phone call, and he and I both know it. He might not be related to the Swedish relatives, but that won't stop him from reaching out. He, unfortunately, knows the family secret and will use it against us if need be."

Well, that's just unfortunate.

This could get bad. Very, very bad, and that scares me to death.

Everett pulls into the clubhouse parking lot nearly an hour later. We drove through town, circled around, and got on one road, then another, before finally going down the one leading to the clubhouse. He barely gets the car in park before my man is storming across the lot, face one of fury.

I open the door and step from within the depths of the sports car, rush to Beast, and wrap my arms around him. The look on his face scares me, and I don't want him to murder his brother.

"Watch out, baby," Beast growls. "I need to kill my little brother."

"No." I hold on tighter and press my face to his chest.

"Sorry, we had to make sure we weren't followed after we got a visit on our way out," Everett remarks, coming around his side of the car.

"Fuck, they came faster than I thought they would." Beast tightens his hold around me. "Let's get the fuck inside." All but lifting me off my feet, Beast guides me into the clubhouse, his brother right behind us.

I'm surprised by how many of Beast's club brothers are standing around, faces hard, looking ready to battle.

"What the fuck took so long?" Reaper demands, coming forward, eyes scanning over me. "You okay?" Concern fills his expression for all of a split second.

"I'm fine, Reaper. I'm just going to go check on my sister and see Ivy and the twins." I tilt my head back and lift on my tip toes as Beast leans down and brushes his lips against mine.

"Don't leave the clubhouse," he orders and lets me go.

"I won't." Assuring him, I step away, give him a small smile, and head for the hallway where I know Ivy will most likely be with the twins, and I'm sure my sister is with them.

CHAPTER 14

BEAST

"How about someone tell me what I'm doing here?" Everett demands the moment Bristol is out of hearing range.

All I want to do right now is go after my woman, take her to my room, and fuck her. I saw the fear in her eyes when I stepped outside and the way she ran to me. Fuck, it felt good to feel her rush to me and wrap her arms around me. Felt like I was her safe place, but I knew she was trying to protect my little brother from getting his ass beat because I didn't know what took them so long.

"Why the fuck didn't you call back to let me know what the hell was going on?" I grind out, turning my attention to my brother. "What the fuck happened?"

"Just Cordell showing up with Ronnie and Bristol's mother as we were leaving. My security was approaching them before anything could happen, but the mother wanted Bristol to come with them, and Cordell gave me his warning. He didn't say anything else, and Ronnie didn't even speak a word," Everett answers. "I don't know if you remember Trace . . ." He pauses long enough for me to nod. Of course, I remember Trace. He was Everett's best friend. "He's head of security in the building and runs the security business that sits on the second floor. He personally took care of them as we were leaving. But still, I wasn't going to take chances that they didn't have someone watching out for us or for them to catch up and follow."

At least my little brother isn't an idiot and knows how to think to protect himself.

"You took your time. Did you have a tail?" Tombstone asks.

"Definitely had someone following," Everett confirms. "Who? I don't know. Blacked-out tinted windows, sedan, no front plates. And no, I didn't say anything to Bristol. I'm not about to freak her out. I don't have to know what she's been through to see the ghost in her eyes."

"Let's sit down, and we'll get down to it on why we

wanted Everett to come to the clubhouse." Reaper grunts, pulls out a chair, and throws himself into it.

"I'm guessing it has something to do with Bristol's sister's husband?" Everett guesses correctly while rolling the sleeves of his dress shirt up to his elbows.

"Giselle is pregnant, and we need to have a restraining order put in place," Reaper says, getting right to it. "The original plan isn't going to work out because we're not about to let the woman be alone without family when she needs it most."

"You want me to handle all of this for you then?" Everett nods, glances around, props his knee on his other leg, and finally meets my gaze head-on. "I'll take care of it. Do you have any evidence for me that will help in starting to build a case against Ronnie?"

"Yeah, we've got the pictures, so does her dad and brother," Scythe remarks. "I have them all here in this file." Holding the said folder out for Everett to take and flip through. "That's all the information I've pulled up on Ronnie and Giselle's marriage so far, including hospital records where she'd had a broken wrist and so on."

I stay silent while my little brother looks through the papers, seeing his jaw tighten and his eyes narrow to thin slits.

"I'll get on this first thing. Restraining order is the first thing. Once the baby is born, we'll have to handle the custody issue. Until then, it's just a matter of keeping him away from her. If he doesn't abide by the order, which I'm sure he won't, I'll nail his ass to the floor. I'll gladly see his ass behind bars."

For the next hour, we all sit around, making plans and discussing the best and worst scenarios for this situation. I keep quiet for most of it, my mind swirling, making plans of my own. There's no way I can let any of this slide. I need to make it known that Bristol is off-limits. I let the club handle the rest with her sister, but where my woman's involved, I'll see to it personally.

If my cousin did indeed make the threat he did, I'm sure he's already made the call out of sheer hatred. Meaning, the Swedish relatives have either already sent someone to the States or they're making plans for coming. Regardless, they're coming, and there's no stopping them.

By the time we finish our conversation, and have a plan in place for Giselle, I'm more than ready to find Bristol, take her to my room, and have my way with her. My cock thickens at the thought of being inside her, and I look damn forward to doing just that, sliding into her slick, wet, tight pussy. Holding her under me while I fuck her however I want to.

"Appreciate you willing to help us out with all of this," Angel says, speaking directly to my brother, holding a hand out for him to shake.

Everett takes Angel's hand in a firm clasp and grins. "It's not a problem at all. I'd have helped out even if my thick-skulled big brother weren't one of you. Bristol is a good woman and works hard keeping me organized and on task, she's also become a friend."

I grit my teeth to keep from snapping at Everett. He's not a friend to my woman, but I know that's a damn lie.

"You've got a plan brewing in that head, brother, I can see the wheels spinning," Diablo remarks gruffly next to me.

I twist in order to face him and cock a brow in question. "What makes you think I've got some plan brewing in my head?"

There's definitely a plan, but it ain't just brewing now. It's setting in stone quickly and firmly. But it involves talking to Bristol first. I'm no longer going to hide who I am from her. Nor my past. We've got enough shit on our plate. We don't need anything else to come between us. I won't allow it to tear her away from me. I nearly let my stupidity get in the way once, and I won't do it again.

"Remember, I know you, Beast, better than anyone else. I can see when the wheels are turning and when you're fuckin' thinking." Diablo snorts, shaking his head, "So, what is it?"

"What is what?" I counter, not ready to talk about

the plan. Not until I've spoken to Bristol first. If I do this, it affects her in a lot of ways, and the target on her back grows even bigger than it already is. Cordell ensured it with the warning he made.

The saying *'If I can't have her, no one can'* comes to mind when I think about the bastard. Last night, he kept quiet in front of the cop, but I'd felt his eyes on me, cool and calculating. He knows what Bristol's worth, but more than that, he knows the threat against me and mine.

"You know what I'm talking about." Diablo cocks a brow of his own and crosses his arms, looking ready to settle in for a massive debate with me which he's known to do. The two of us can go toe to toe with each other and talk about shit, debating it until the end of time, always pointing out different views on whatever it is we're talking about. But that's what makes him my best friend.

"Nothing to talk about, at least not yet," I admit, not having time for the argumentized debate. "I'll let you know when I have it confirmed and go for it."

Diablo holds my gaze and stares at me for a long moment before he blinks and nods. "It's got to do with Bristol, and you want to talk to her first, am I right?"

"Yup," I grunt and cock my head slightly, feeling my neck pop. The sound of a loud cracking noise fills my head, and it feels damn good.

"Then I'll let you get to your woman. I expect to hear this plan of yours tonight." Diablo chuckles, drops his arms, and moves toward my little brother and the others, shouting out Everett's name. "Since you're my brother's brother, that makes you mine."

I can't help but snort at Diablo's remark. Since the beginning, when we first met on the streets, we've been brothers. We've been brothers by the streets and brothers by the club. He's my family, same as those who wear the same patch as me. I guess he's about to make Everett also a part of the family. I'm not sure how I should feel about it, but I'll figure it out later.

Now, it's time to find Bristol and talk to her, see what she thinks. First things first, fuck her in my bed like I've wanted to for so damn long.

Bristol said she was going to be with Ivy and her sister, so I make my way to the room Reaper had set up as a gaming room/playroom for the kids. It's where Ivy can normally be found unless she's either with Reaper or in their room.

Stepping into the room, my brows furrow, and I don't see Bristol. "Where's Bristol?"

Ivy and Giselle both look at me in confusion.

"I thought she was at work," Giselle utters quietly.

"Everett brought her to the clubhouse two hours ago. She didn't come in here?" My gut tightens as different scenarios start swirling around in my head.

"No," Ivy answers, looking concerned.

Reaper comes up beside me. "Looking for Bristol?" he asks, raising a brow.

"Yeah," I say, turning to him. "You know where she's at?"

"Yep," he answers, moves to Ivy, and pulls her in his arms. "Time to go home, Princess."

"Where is she?" I don't like the way my Prez answered that.

Reaper hits me with a glare. "Why don't you tell me why a woman I see as a little sister, a part of my family, would escape the clubhouse only moments after saying she was going to find Ivy and Giselle? Bristol took one of the four-wheelers and took off into the woods. A little bit later, she stepped into the house, and I'm willing to bet she's in her room where, if I remember correctly, is where she would always go when escaping whatever is bothering her."

My anger rises at the cynical way my Prez said this, but I bite my tongue to keep from disrespecting him.

"Want to know why she did this?" Reaper asks, his tone darkening.

"Why?" I grit out, feeling my jaw tighten more and my gut twisting.

"Because one of the PPs was caught going in and out of your room," he answers. "Now, we're heading home. If you're coming with, you best be ready to handle Bristol with care 'cause it wasn't just any PP that was on the footage I saw before coming in this room. It was Jezebel."

Oh fucking kill me. I knew fucking the bitch that first time was a bad idea. Since then, she's been trying to get my attention any chance she can. This is the last thing I need right now on top of everything else. "I'll deal with that bitch later. Right now, I'm following you, getting my woman, and then going home."

'Cause without knowing what the hell happened between Bristol and Jezebel, I can't bring her back to my room. Fuck I need to just send a prospect to get me a new bed along with sheets and a comforter. At least then, Bristol will know that she's the only woman who's been in my bed and on the new sheets.

CHAPTER 15

BRISTOL

I didn't make it to my sister or Ivy as I intended to. I'd made the mistake of stopping at Beast's room and finding a woman there naked. I recognized her immediately as one of the skanks who are known around here as the pocket pussies or whatever they're called, and she informed me how much she enjoyed Beast after he dropped me off at work. She claimed he would never get his fill with just me and that I needed to get used to it. The way she said this, getting out of his bed, looking freshly fucked, I felt the betrayal slashing at my insides, destroying me.

I didn't say anything, though I'm sure I should have. Instead, I slipped out the back, making sure no one saw me. Considering I didn't have my car, I took one of the four-wheelers Ivy and the others have here at the clubhouse to ride around on. I'd been on them before and knew how to ride one and headed straight through the woods, not stopping until I made it to Reaper and Ivy's house. I still have a key and let myself inside, where I went to my old room.

Now, lying here, I've done nothing but let the tears stream down my face. The pain of seeing that woman . . . of knowing she's right . . . it all comes flooding through my system like a tidal wave.

I don't want to believe what that skank said, but she'd been in Beast's bed. Hair mused, her face looking all too pleased by being caught, and her body looked way better than mine. Where I have scars, she's flawless.

Of course, any man would find her sexy because she's not damaged goods. She's not been violated as I have.

Tears spill, and a sob breaks through what little hold I have left on the anguish inside me. Curling more into myself, I hate what I'm feeling and why, but I can't help it.

I wish I could be everything Beast needs, but I'm not. Even I can sense he's gentle with me even when he's taking me hard. He doesn't lose his control while fucking me. I've heard the stories about what he's like in bed. Plenty of women have bragged about being taken by him like a beast rather than a man. He's rough and wild in bed, but not once has he been either with me. So, it can only mean one thing. I don't think I'm enough to give him what he needs, and because of this, he'd go to one of those women to get it.

My heart breaks at the thought. It truly tears me into pieces, coming to realize all of this. Why couldn't I be enough for him?

I barely register the sound of the rumbling roar of a motorcycle pulling into the driveway. It's Ivy and Reaper's house. I'm used to the sound from when I lived here. I don't know what came over me to come here, but it's home. Both Ivy and Reaper made it so it's my home too. I guess that would explain why I needed to come here. It's the first place I ever felt I belong. They didn't just treat me like I was some victim. Ivy saw to it that I knew I wasn't. Reaper made certain I felt welcomed and that I was family regardless of not sharing blood.

So many years ago, right after I turned eighteen, he hired me at Keeper's Pub, giving me my first job. He didn't have to take the chance on me, but he did. For that, I'll always be thankful because it meant freedom. Freedom from the life I didn't want.

"Woman, you want to explain to me what the fuck you're doing here and not at the clubhouse?"

The voice attached to the question has me jumping

in shock and surprise. I stare at Beast with wide eyes for the first time seeing him pissed off. I don't think I've ever seen him like this. Sure, he's been irritated and frustrated, but never this.

"What are you doing here, Beast?" I ask, licking my dry lips nervously.

"Came to get you," he growls, his voice nearly animalistic, stepping closer to the bed, hand reaching out in my direction. "Come on, let's get out of here."

"I don't want to go anywhere with you," I whisper, my heart aching. The pain of what I felt, the betrayal, it's agonizing.

"Baby, you either come with me peacefully, or I throw you over my shoulder and take you out of here. Either way, we're leaving here together and going the fuck home."

My mouth parts in a silent gasp, and my eyes widen. He can't be serious right now.

"Beast, just go." Shaking my head, I turn away from him. "I don't want to talk to you right now."

"Too bad," he states in one second and the next, I find myself up and over his shoulder.

"Beast," I gasp, "put me down." I try to push myself upright, but unfortunately, I don't have the upper arm strength to do it.

"Not gonna happen."

Moving through the house, Beast doesn't say

another word as he stalks through the door and out to the bike, where he finally sets me down with my ass planted on the back. Deciding to play it smart, I don't bother trying to get off as he gets on in front of me. I figure I'll get away from him whenever we get where he's taking me.

He said home. Does that mean he's taking me to my house? If so, I'll scoop up Jagger and go hole up in my room.

Beast settles in front of me, turns his bike on, adjusts the heavy machinery between his legs, and kicks up the kickstand. Tense, I wrap my arms around Beast's waist, not wanting him to order me to do so or force me closer, and he doesn't do either, thankfully.

On the back of Beast's bike, I find a moment of peace, feeling the fresh air and the wind whipping around us. Every time I'm on the back of his bike it feels amazing. There's nowhere else I would rather be. It sucks that the ride is shorter than I would have liked. In no time, Beast is pulling up at the house, mine, of course, and parks just outside the backdoor.

I should say something to him about parking wherever he sees fit in my yard. I mean, I have a garage for a reason. I also have a flipping driveway.

I climb off the back of his bike, not waiting for him as I stomp over to the door, unlock it using the key I happen to have put in my pocket, and step into the house. I barely get through the entrance when I feel Beast's heat at my back. He moves quickly, gripping my arm and twirling me around to face him while pressing me against the wall right next to where the door closes.

"Beast, let me go," I murmur, unsure of what he's trying to prove.

"I don't think so, woman, I'm tired of the bullshit. You always running and hiding. Always pushing me away rather than talkin' to me," he snarls, getting in my face, his body leaving no space between the two of us.

"Maybe I do it out of self-preservation." I breathe, my breast brushing against his chest.

"Bullshit, you do it because you're damn scared of what we've got, and I'm done letting you run. You ain't running from me anymore," he says just before slamming his mouth to mine. His tongue plunges in and demands control. One hand holds me still at the waist while the other moves and tangles my hair in a tightening grip that should scare me, but it doesn't.

In fact, it does the complete opposite. Between my legs, I can feel the moisture seeping from my entrance, soaking my panties. It's total lunacy I would be wet because of him controlling me like this, but I am.

Beast moves and lifts me until I have no other choice but to wrap myself around him. Moving through the house, Beast carries me to my bedroom and leans forward until my back is to the mattress.

Breaking his lips from mine, he jerks back, rips my shirt open, and all but shreds my pants from my body, leaving me in the lacy bra and panty match set I picked out this morning.

Without a word, he keeps his gaze firmly on my body, lust burning in those dark orbs of his, and he doesn't hide it. This isn't the man who's been having sex with me. No, it's the one within the man, the one that makes him Beast.

"Beast," I whisper, earning that dark gaze of his.

I watch closely as his nostrils flare, eyes ablaze, and he strips off his cut, the shoulder holster he wears, and his shirt. Next, he toes off his boots and undoes his belt. Rather than tossing his belt with his shirt, he leans over me, grabs both my arms, lifts them over my head, and uses the belt to secure them there.

"Leave them where they are," he commands. "You move them, I'll make you pay."

"Wh-what are you doing?" The question comes out no more than a breath.

"Teaching you a lesson," he answers and rolls me to my stomach. "Teaching you that you don't run from me. You don't let skanks try and destroy what we've got. And you sure as fuck don't . . ." Beast lifts my hips until my ass is in the air, "leave the safety of the clubhouse without me knowing about it." The words barely leave his mouth before I feel the first sharp pain against my ass and squeal.

"Did you just spank me?" I blurt the question out, completely shocked that he'd do something like that.

"Damn right I did," he states and does it again to the other side of my ass. "You're gonna learn who you fuckin' belong to, Bristol."

Oh my God.

Several times he spanks me, never in the same spot, and each time he rubs his hands over the spot he's just swatted. Between my legs aches, and I don't understand it. I didn't know being spanked could be a turn-on, but with the way he's doing it, swatting my ass, dipping down to trail his fingers through my juice and then back again, it's insanity.

By the time he shifts between my legs, I'm a panting mess. With my arms locked together with his belt, I can't hold myself upright.

"Your pussy's fuckin' drenched right now, Bristol."

A shiver rushes over me, through me. I don't know how to explain it, but it's exhilarating. Especially when he uses his tongue to swipe through my slit and plunges inside me. It intensifies when he gives a groan of approval. His mouth on me, him eating me, it's like I'll come at any second. That is until he pulls back, and the feeling disappears.

"You're not about to come yet," he states, blowing a breath over my clit.

"Beast," I whimper, the sensations overwhelming me.

"You come when I say you do, Bristol, not a moment before." Beast returns his mouth to what he was doing, driving me insane.

I don't know how many times he drove me to the brink of release only to pull away. Sweat beads my body, and I feel the trembles throughout my body. I want to come, but Beast refuses to allow me this, even when I plead for him to let me.

A whimper leaves my throat as Beast draws away and rolls me over, lifts my legs to his shoulders, and surges forward, his cock slamming inside me. A scream rips from my chest, and I arch into him, taking the pounding of his cock fucking into me like a jackhammer. Each thrust is hard, ruthless, and unforgiving. More than that, it's everything I ever wanted to feel from him.

"Fuckin' love this pussy," he states harshly. "Love how tight you feel around me. The way your pussy walls clench and suck me right in. It's the best feeling in the world. Now, come for me, Bristol. Come on my cock, baby. Squeeze me as only you can do."

As if on command, my release overcomes me, and I cry out his name, wishing I could touch him. Beast joins me with a grunt of his own, and his thrusts never slow. He keeps going, powering through his orgasm.

"We're nowhere near done, baby, don't think we are. I'm fuckin' you until you know just who you belong to and know that I'd never fuck you over," he says and dips down to claim my lips.

I don't need him to keep going to know who I belong to, but does that mean he belongs to me too? God, I hope so because it'll hurt if it's not true.

CHAPTER 16

BEAST

"I didn't know that bitch was in my room when you went in there." It still pisses me off who was in there in the first place, and I intend to find out why, but Bristol comes first, and making sure she's okay is far more important.

I lost my mind thinking of the possibilities on the way to get her, and then fucked her until she passed out from the pleasure I spent the night giving her. It was heavily intoxicating hearing her screams of pleasure. What I did with her, I've been wanting to do since the first moment I saw her when she started working at Keeper's Pub. I had a plan for when I finally got inside her.

When it comes to Bristol, she deserves everything.

To feel special and be loved in a bed. So that's what I intended to keep in this bed with her. I also know she'd love me fucking her dirty and that's what I'd planned for at the clubhouse. However, shit keeps happening, and I couldn't hold myself back any longer.

Bristol makes me lose my control, and I needed to show her who was in charge in this relationship. I wasn't going to let her fuck us up because of something that didn't happen.

"If you didn't know, then how did she get in your room?" Bristol whispers, her fingers trailing over my stomach, toying with the hairs leading downward.

I don't miss the hurt in her voice, and it enrages me. "I don't fuckin' know how she got in my room, but I intend to find out. Those bitches at the clubhouse know the rules for them being there. They know what's off limits, and the bitch never should have been in my room without my permission."

"Don't you lock your room?" Lifting her head, she meets my gaze with a furrowed brow, concern filling her expression.

"Yeah, normally I do. I had to have forgotten to lock it back up after being in there earlier before you got to the clubhouse," I answer, lifting my head enough to brush my lips against hers. "If I had locked it, you wouldn't have been able to get in there, let alone Jezebel. She never would have been about to fuck with you the way she did if I hadn't left the damn door unlocked."

"She was naked, looking as if she'd been very pleased with herself." I could hear the hurt in Bristol's voice, and it guts me to know that because of my fuck up, some bitch was able to hurt her.

"I'm sorry, Butterfingers, but I was never with her."

"But you have been with her. Jezebel was kind enough to tell me how you and she had a great time the night you got back," she says, anguish filling her voice and gutting me at the same time.

"Bristol, I can't change shit that happened before I got my head out of my ass. I fucked up when it comes to you in more ways than I care to admit, but we're past all that now and can't be looking in the rearview mirror constantly. You gotta let it go, and so do I." The both of us need to let all the shit in the past go and move on. And that means it's time to explain to her my plan to put a stop to the Swedish relatives from fucking with me or getting her.

"I can let it go," she whispers, nodding, "but I've got to admit, I'm tired of hearing those women talk about your cock and how well you know how to use it. Even more about how you fucked them while—"

"Don't worry about what those bitches say. From now on, it's just you and me. My cock in your pussy. Your pussy taking what I give it and how I want to give it. When. Where. Doesn't matter long as my cock's inside you," I state firmly, not letting her finish her sentence. Rolling her until I'm between her legs and she's on her back, I slip through her slick heat and slide right into the sweetest pussy I've ever known. "When it comes to you and me, this is all that matters. Not what some skank says or tries to pull over on you. They're just trying to get in your head. You can't let them do that. So, I'm gonna fuck you until all you can think about is feeling me inside you."

"Oh . . . Beast." Her voice breaks on a moan, driving me insane with the headiness of it. So many things about this woman turn me on, and her voice is definitely one of them. Each and every sound that comes from her mouth makes me want to fuck her, and being inside her, it makes me want to fuck her even more. I intend to do that now.

After I have my fill for now and sate the lust inside me that only she can tame, I'll fill her in on what needs to happen.

"You can't be serious?" Bristol gapes, staring at me wide-eyed.

"Very serious," I grumble. "When it comes to keeping you safe, I'll do what it takes."

"But this?" She blinks, shaking her head. "I think you've lost some marbles if you think this is a good idea."

"What better way to get the bastards to leave us alone?" Shrugging, I get out of bed, find my jeans on the floor, and have to pick Jagger up off them before I can pull them on. Tossing the cat on the bed, I meet Bristol's gaze while shoving one leg and then the other in my jeans. "If we don't, then they'll keep coming at us until they get what they want."

"But to fake our deaths? That's complete insanity." She huffs, pulling the sheet over her breasts to conceal them from my view at the same time pulling Jagger toward her. "We can't just fake our deaths. Besides, wouldn't they go after your brother if they thought you were dead?"

"No, because he wasn't born first," I inform her. "There's no other way around this."

"There has to be. We can't do this. Seriously, Beast, there's no way possible to do it. It's also way, way, way illegal. We can't do something so asinine and get away with it."

"We can if we have the right connections." Crossing my arms, I stand firm. I'm not going to change my mind on this.

"There has to be another way," Bristol cries. "We don't have to hide from them . . ." She pauses, and I can all but hear the wheels spinning in her head. "What if . . . what if we got married? Wouldn't that put a stop to it?"

"They'd come after our kid then if we did that." The thought of her being pregnant scares the shit out of me. We haven't been using protection, and I know she's not on the pill. I asked her about it the first time we had sex. We've been playing with fire, but when it comes to sex with my woman, I don't want any barriers, and considering she's not on anything, I'm willing to bet she's already knocked up. If not, then she will be soon enough.

"We can protect a child together," she protests hastily. "I won't do this, Beast. We can't. It's not the right way to handle this. I know in my heart it's not the right way. It would mean disappearing from those we see as family. I started to gain a relationship with my sister."

"I know, baby." I blow out a frustrated breath, close my eyes, and pinch the bridge of my nose. "It's not going to be easy, I know it, but it would work." She'd be safe, and I could make sure they never found either of us.

I knew what it would mean, and it would suck.

"I'm not doing it, Beast," she declares, getting out of the bed and glaring at me. "You can do it all you want, but I refuse to do so. If you want to fake your death, then by all means, go for it." Standing across from the bed, gloriously naked, nipples hard and her body flush from the fucking I'd given her, she stands off with me. "If you do this, you'll be nothing more than a coward," she snaps, spins on her heels, stomps the short distance to the bathroom, and slams the door behind her.

Nothing more than a coward. That's the way she would see me if I did this, but it would mean protecting her and keeping her from being taken from me.

"Fuck," I breathe out harshly, raking my fingers through my hair roughly. She thinks there's a better way to handle this situation. Maybe there is but damned if I can figure it out. One thing I know for certain, though, is she's right, it is a coward's move. I just don't want to lose her.

Again.

If I'm going to be able to keep everything I have in my life. My family. My woman. I'm going to need to come up with a way to make sure no one can take what's mine from me. This means I'll need to talk to my brothers. With their help maybe I can see that nothing ever happens to Bristol or anyone else I care about.

CHAPTER 17

BRISTOL

I can't believe him. How could he come up with something so foolish as faking deaths . . . his and mine. I refuse to let him do this. I won't do it.

Quickly I take a shower, scrubbing harshly at my skin . . . totally infuriated with what he claims he wants us to do. No flipping way it is happening. Last night, he spent the entire night inside me, forcing me to admit that I belong to him. Now, he came up with something so idiotic as this. I don't care if his family is full of weirdos who think they can demand something from anyone. Just because they're from a royal line and think their shit doesn't stink doesn't mean the bed of roses they sleep in doesn't have the same smell as any other slimeball.

I won't let the insufferable male ego Beast seems to have do something so asinine as this. It's not about to happen. I don't care if I have to tattle on him to Reaper and Angel. They'll make sure he doesn't do this.

Sure, I don't want to fake our deaths and disappear after I've finally gotten my sister in my life. But that's not the reason for this. I don't want to leave a life where I'm finally getting everything I ever wanted. A family. Beast. Happiness. Not just contentment. I was holding something far more precious to me than just that. I was holding my future, and I refuse to allow Beast to throw what we have now away.

Finishing my shower, I turn the water off and step out, only to come to a stop at the sight of Beast standing there leaning against the counter, holding my towel up for me.

"I locked the door to keep you out," I mutter, stepping toward him to take the big fluffy towel.

"A lock won't keep me away from you, Butterfingers. You should know that by now," he states with that matter-of-fact tone in his voice.

"Whatever."

Turning away from him, I wrap the towel around my body and stomp back into the bedroom, trying to ignore him. It's not an easy feat by any means. Beast is one of those men you can't get by without noticing. It's one of the things that's always drawn me to him. That and the fact he makes me laugh. Still, I'm not going to let him get away with this without giving him the cold shoulder.

"I'll talk to Reaper and the others."

Those words coming from his mouth cause me to pause in my attempt to freeze him out.

"What did you say?" I ask, slowly turning to face Beast.

"I'm gonna talk to the club, figure something else out," he answers, knowing eyes boring into me. "You're right, and I shouldn't have asked you to do something like this."

My breath catches in my chest, and I tighten my grip on the front of the towel, holding it secure while his words sink in. I watch him closely while he closes the short distance between us.

Beast's hands curl around either side of my waist, pulling me in close at the same time, dipping his head lower to rest his forehead against mine. "You mean more to me than anything or one could ever mean in my life, Bristol. I lose you, baby, they might as well put a bullet in me 'cause I wouldn't be able to breathe without you. I love you too damn much to classify it as actual love. It doesn't even begin to describe what exactly I feel for you."

"You love me?" My vision becomes blurry, making it difficult to see past the unshed tears.

"More than you'll ever know, Butterfingers." Those lips of his brush mine with each word. Not quite in a kiss, but enough that I want nothing more.

"I feel the same." Breath hitching, I lean in, dropping my hand from the towel that I tucked around my body to clench at either side of his shoulders, holding onto him to keep my knees from collapsing beneath me.

"I know." Beast scoops me into his arms and carries me back over to the bed, lays me down, and comes over me, claiming my mouth with his.

The towel is pulled away from my body, and he takes his time to explore every inch of me, driving me wild like we hadn't just spent the night and morning having sex. It's beautiful, breathtaking, more than a little intoxicating. Without his touch, I'd never be the same, and I know it.

After yet another shower, this time spent with Beast in the cubical with me. His cock slipping inside me while holding me up with my back pressed to the tile wall, we finally get dressed and head to the clubhouse.

The moment we pull into the clubhouse, my stomach tightens at the sight of the amount of police cars and tactical vehicles in the parking area. To make matters worse, my mother, Ronnie, and Cordell are standing toward the back. A smug look on my mother's face doesn't sit well with me. The only thing keeping me from losing it is that Beast seems calm while he parks and shuts the bike off.

"Come on, baby, let's go find out what the hell's going on here," he says, tapping my leg. "I see my brother's car is already here, so we don't have to call him to deal with whatever the fuck we're about to walk into."

"I don't have a good feeling about this." A sense of despair eats at my stomach, knowing it's because of me this is happening.

"Bristol, it's going to be okay, baby, I promise."

I nod, wanting more than anything to believe him, but it scares me that anything at all would be happening like this, as it were. Getting off the back of the bike, I don't have to wait long for him to follow suit, and he wraps his arm around my shoulders. Together, we ignore the presence of those in the parking lot and head into the clubhouse. If Beast's arm wasn't already around me, I might have stumbled at the tension filling the room.

Guilt threatens to consume me, but I don't allow it. If I do, then I'll never be able to forgive myself. Right now, I need to stay strong, not just for me but for those here that I see as family.

Sitting on a few of the couches on the other side of the room, across from where all the tables are situated, the ol' ladies surround my sister. Ivy and Sutton, on either side of her, holding her hands. I want to go to them, but I stay next to Beast, needing his support more at the moment. At least until I know exactly what's happening.

"Beast." The cop from the other night nods as he steps forward.

"Bryant," Beast grunts, his displeasure filling his deep baritone. Moving past the officer, Beast stops next to Reaper, Angel, Diablo, and a few others, as well as my boss, and asks, "What's going on here?"

"They got a warrant to search the place for Giselle." Reaper grunts and jerks his chin in the direction of my sister. "We told them we had nothing to hide. It's a good thing her attorney was here this morning with her. It helped speed things along."

"That's good," I mumble and look at Everett with a small smile, then back to the others. "Why are all the police still here?"

"It wasn't just her they were searching for," Diablo answered, his lip curling in disgust.

"What?" That feeling in my stomach worsens as I wait for someone to explain.

"I've got this under control," Everett remarks, shaking his head. "It was reported you were being held and not in the right state of mind. That you needed to be given to your mother for your protection. It's bullshit, and the officers here just needed to speak with you before leaving."

"I'm going to kill her," I mutter to myself.

"Darlin', I'd keep things like that to myself if I were you." Angel snorts. "Don't need to give the men in blue a reason to take you in."

"This is not cool," I snap huffingly, letting my anger get the best of me. Turning toward the nearest officer, I step out of Beast's grasp, hands planted on my waist, and give him my best glare.

"Oh no," Giselle gasps loudly.

I ignore her as I focus on the police officers. I recognize him from my time working at Keeper's Pub. He's a nice guy with a wife who I know he'd bring with him. She's nice and always filled with laughter. I just don't remember their names right now. "Do I look like I'm not in the right head space?" I don't give him a chance to answer as I keep going. "To answer that, yes, I am. I'm perfectly fine, and so is my sister." I point in her direction. "You all need to get your facts straight rather than storming in here the way you have and disrupting these people's day the way you have. The reason you're all here is because my mother is a self-absorbed bitch who needs her head examined. She refuses to allow it to sink into her pea-brained head that I'm not going to bend to her will or do as she demands. I'm well over eighteen and have been on my own since the same age. I do not need this, and neither does Giselle."

"Ma'am, we're just trying to get everything taken care of," the officer says, his lips twitching in amusement. "We've already spoken with your sister and her lawyer. Got the paperwork for the restraining order. We just needed to speak to you. Reaper assured us you would be in sometime soon. Everyone here has vouched for you, as well as your boss here." Jerking his chin up, he outright grins. "Those of us here know this club. We might not see eye to eye with them all the damn time, but we know they're protective and will do what it takes to help those who need it. We also know you from working at the Keeper's Pub. So, we also know you and know that shit with the woman outside is bullshit. I'd suggest getting a restraining order against her."

"Already done," Everett mutters, holding a paper outward. "It's against all three of those idiots outside."

"Well, then, that's good to know." The officer takes the paper from him, scans over it, and hands it back. "We'll get out of here, but if I were you, I'd get Giselle away from here. Especially considering the information you've divulged."

I suck in a breath, not liking the meaning behind

that, but I know deep down he's right. No matter how much I want to keep my sister close, she needs to disappear, at least for a little while.

Beast pulls me back in his arms and turns me so I can bury my face in his chest. I want nothing more than to go back to this morning when we were still in bed, and it was just the two of us.

What will happen next?

To make it easier on the club, we need to find somewhere to send my sister. Then, figure out what's going on with the people Beast wanted to fake our deaths to hide from.

Is it even possible for us to find peace and not worry about what will happen next?

CHAPTER 18

BEAST

Hours later, and I'm still fuming over the bullshit move Bristol's mother tried pulling here. Ronnie couldn't give a damn about Giselle. He sees her as property and wants her back, but he's smart enough he wouldn't go up against the club in such a way. Knowing him, he'd have done something different. Much different. Shadier, if possible.

After Bristol's outburst earlier, everyone that wasn't an ol' lady or member of the club made a hasty exit. Even the PPs went and hid back in their rooms, though they made it known they'd be around if needed.

Bristol didn't see it, but I did with the way Jezebel gave me the come fuck me look, which is good because that's the last thing she needs to deal with right now.

More fucking drama. My brothers and I will handle her first thing before getting to the heart of the rest of the bullshit happening.

Which is what we're about to do. The women finally settled down, and Bristol isn't on the verge of another freakout. Looking back on it still pisses me off because she should never have had to lose her shit the way she did. She's been through a lot, and even with what Potter did to her, she didn't lose it like that. That right there makes me want to commit murder. Unfortunately, that's something I can't do. Not without coming up with a damn good way of making it happen and not letting fingers be turned our way. Maybe I could pin it on Cordell or Ronnie. Make things simple for everyone around.

An idea pops into my head, and I grin at the very thought. It would do them good to get what they deserve. The new plan forming in my head would not only eliminate the threat those three are making, but also that of my other problems. Kill two birds with one stone. But we'd have to get the timing right.

I'd also have to make sure that my woman never found out that we were involved in it in any way. She might hate her mother, but that doesn't mean she'd want her dead.

Stepping into church, I take my seat and wait for

everyone else to join me. Reaper's already there, and I jerk my chin up in acknowledgment.

"We need to do something about Jezebel," I inform him as the last of my brothers fill the room.

"Bristol tell you what all happened?" Reaper asks, cocking a brow.

"Yeah, stupid bitch put thoughts in my woman's head about her not being enough for me. But more than that. She was in my room. I fucked up and didn't lock my room back up as I should have, and she went in there. She hurt Bristol, and I won't let that slide. Bristol has been through e-fuckin-nough." The words vibrate in my chest as I speak and slam my fist on the table. "I want her gone that way she can't fuck with Bristol anymore."

"I agree," Diablo remarks, nodding. "Don't get me wrong, I love the easy pussy, but what she did was fucked up. If she'll do it, what's to say the others don't follow suit and try shit like that. She knew better than to go in Beast's room without being with him or told to."

"What I'd like to know is what the hell she was doing in there in the first place?" Styxx sneers. "She was in there a good while before Bristol even went to Beast's room."

"I have to say it's sketchy to me as well." Tombstone nods. "We've had enough problems when it comes to bitches like her around here."

"Take Claws for one and her crazy ass sister who wasn't even one of the clubwhores around here," Angel growls, flexing his fingers and bawling them into fists. "Last thing we need is another bitch around here going psycho on us."

"Guess there's no reason to call for a vote on this one," Reaper states, glancing around the table with hard eyes. When no one objects, Reaper nods. "Azrael, you and Cerberus go grab the bitch and bring her in here. First and foremost, we're going to find out what the fuck she was doing in Beast's room before Bristol walked in there, and depending on what she says will depend on if we let her go or lock her down at the cabin. I'm not taking chances with this kind of shit anymore. Not when we still have to deal with the Scarlet Needles on top of everything else going on." Finishing that statement, Reaper looks directly at me. "This shit is getting out of hand with Bristol's mother. We need to put a stop to it."

"How can we do that without it coming back on the club?" Thanatos grunts. "Bitch is obviously from money."

"Why do you say that?" Leaning back in my seat, I focus on the other man, seeing the way he's grinding his teeth together. "Her family is also from money; she's got that behind her."

"What she's got is in name only," Scythe answers rather than Thanatos, getting everyone's attention.

"The fuck does that mean?" Hellhound demands, straightening in his chair.

"Means she's broke and only has ties to the family name," I remark, not liking this at all. This has got to be the reason she's so hard up on getting ahold of Bristol's trust fund.

"Scythe, what have you found?" Reaper growls.

"Nothing anyone in here's gonna like hearing," he answers as Azrael opens the door and drags in a smug-looking Jezebel. Cerberus comes in behind, closing the door. Neither man takes a seat, instead, they stand with the bitch between them.

"Am I here to give you guys a show?" Jezebel all but purrs, glancing around the table, eyeing each of us before stopping her gaze on me and licking her lips. "I don't mind if you guys need some entertainment in here."

"What were you doing in a brother's room without his permission?" Prez demands coolly, keeping his voice calm.

Jezebel didn't remove her gaze from mine as she smiles and answers. "I thought Beast would like to have some fun. He hadn't been around, and I figured

I'd surprise him. I knocked on his door and found it unlocked. That's when I decided to surprise him. I didn't know his woman would come in there. If I'd had the slightest idea, I wouldn't have gone in there. I know the rules." Her voice grates on my nerves with the way she's trying to act all innocent.

"If you know the rules, then you know that you're not allowed in those rooms until asked for or told to go in there." Angel sneers.

"I'm sorry," she murmurs, losing the smile and looking to the head of the table. "I really didn't mean anything by it. Honestly."

I glance around, seeing the looks on my brothers' faces and wonder if they're buying this shit.

Scythe leans forward, raps his knuckles on the table, and cocks a brow at the clubwhore. "You were in his room for a while before Bristol walked in there. What were you doing?"

"I stripped out of my clothes and got in Beast's bed to wait for him," she responds, and I get the feeling there's more to it. She's playing games. I can feel it. What that game is I'm not sure yet.

"So, why is it, that no sooner you left his room, you made a call to Cordell Barker?" Scythe questions, watching the bitch knowingly dropping that bit of information that doesn't surprise me in the least, though it should.

When it doesn't, only because I should have seen it coming, especially with what my brother said about the warning Cordell gave him yesterday.

Cocking a brow, I slowly look back to the bitch in question and get to my feet. "Tell me, Jezebel, how did you get hooked up with Cordell? Or were you working with him for other reasons?" Anger surges through my veins, but I keep myself calm to keep from losing my shit.

"I don't know what you're talking about," she says, visibly tensing.

"Don't bullshit us, bitch, and tell us what the fuck you're playing at here." My gut is telling me there's more to it. "And don't bother lying. It'll only make things worse for you."

Jezebel loses that fearful look and narrows her gaze to a glare. Her lip curls in disgust. "Since you seem to have it all figured out, you can just figure out the rest of it," she says and tries to struggle against the grip Azrael has on her. "I won't tell you anything else."

"We'll see about that," Reaper states, coming out of his seat. "Azrael, Cerberus, take her to the cabin. We'll deal with her later and get answers. We've got some other things to handle besides her and don't have time to deal with her ass right now."

"Taking me anywhere isn't going to stop what's about to happen." Jezebel laughs.

"And what would that be?" That feeling in my gut isn't sitting well with me. Not in the least bit. Stepping close to the bitch, I hold her gaze. "What do you know is going to happen?" I demand, pulling a knife from its sheath and pressing it against her slender neck.

"Why should I tell you when I know you're just going to kill me anyway?" The sneer that forms on her lips contorts her expression to one of pure hatred.

"Reason you tell us anything is to keep us from dragging your death out," Tombstone remarks harshly. "You want us to bury you alive? Force you to suffocate and choke on the dirt sealing you in the ground? Or better yet, seal you in a tomb with your worst nightmare."

"You can't do anything to me without repercussions," Jezebel scoffs.

"That's what you think." I sneer and get right in her face while pressing the blade harder, the tip breaking skin. "I've no problem slitting your throat, so you might as well start talking because if you don't, you'll go through hell before you take your last breath."

"*Förrädarenson,*" Jezebel spits and leans in on the blade. "That's what you are, and you will pay in the worst way possible. They'll see to it. Cordell will have what's his, and you will suffer. You have many enemies, and they all want in on the action of taking you all out. Each and every one of you for getting in their way."

"Take her to the cabin," Reaper snarls the command, more than done with what the bitch is saying. "Finish getting information out of her there."

"You got it, Prez." Azrael grunts, dragging Jezebel back away from the blade I was holding to her neck.

No one speaks as the two men remove Jezebel completely from the room. The tension is thick in the air and makes me feel uneasy.

"Before they brought her," Scythe is the first to speak up, "I found a connection between Bristol's mother and the Scarlet Needles."

"Fuck," Angel snarls. "What's the connection?"

"Still looking more into that, but if I had to guess, the mother was going to use the trust fund to secure her place within the group. This has become more than just about Bristol and Giselle. It involves the Scarlet Needles, and they still have contracts out on the women," Scythe announces.

"Then it's time we plan to make sure that the bitch can't get her hands on Bristol, Giselle, or either of their funds," Diablo states.

"Gonna be hard for us to ensure Giselle's trust," Thanatos states, clasping his hands together as he leans forward, bracing his elbows on the table. "She told me that Ronnie forced her to sign it over to him. I'm willing to bet that he's also involved in this."

That's something I was afraid of.

"I have an idea that might ensure she gets her money back," I mutter, retaking my seat.

"What's the idea?" Reaper growls.

Taking a breath, I tell them my thoughts on what we should do in order to see that nothing comes back on us, but also takes care of the situation. Several of my brothers put input in as I finished filling them in on the idea. By the time I'm finished talking, I know without the vote, that my brothers are with me on this. The remainder of church is spent fine-tuning everything we can in order to make it happen.

Leaving the room, I still feel the tension, the tightening in my gut, but I know I've got my brothers at my back. Together, we'll do what it takes to ensure the safety of not just my woman but all of them.

CHAPTER 19

BRISTOL

I don't know if I should be nervous, worried, or maybe scared when Beast and the others file out of church. The look on his face is one of fury, and it is enough to cause me to suck in a breath when our eyes meet.

I want to blame myself for whatever he's thinking. It's my family that's causing the issues going on right now. Not my brother or dad, but my mother and I hate to say it, my sister. Though I can fully put the blame on my mother. My sister couldn't help that she needed help to get away from the monster my mother strapped her with.

Keeping focus solely on Beast, I watch him all but prowl in my direction. I don't know what happened while in there, but I saw Azrael and Cerberus come out of there and go back in with Jezebel. A short while later, they came back out. The woman had blood at her neck, and the two men carted her out of the clubhouse. That didn't stop her from seeing me and glaring at me. I think if she could have, she'd have killed me in that moment, and I want to know why.

I'm getting the feeling something more is going on here, I just don't know what. Hopefully, Beast will tell me something and not leave me in the dark.

The instant Beast is close enough, he wraps an arm around my waist and dips his head down to press his forehead against the top of my head.

Licking my lips, I tilt my head back until we're nose to nose and ask, "What's going on?" I'm not waiting around for answers, I want to know what the hell is going on. More than that, I want to make sure he's not going to go through with the idiotic plan of faking our deaths. He said he wasn't, and I need to know he's not.

"Lots of shit happenin', Butterfingers," he mutters, releasing a heavy breath and stepping back. "Come on." Dropping his hands from my waist, he takes my hand. "Let's go to my room and talk in there."

Wordlessly, I follow him, my stomach tightening as my nerves threaten to overtake me with my fears of what's to come. It doesn't help I'm still reeling over the fact the police were here at the clubhouse along with my mother.

There's something else going on. I can all but feel it. Something big is about to happen.

Beast unlocks and opens the door to his room. Together, we step in, and he closes the door behind us, closing us in, alone in a room that only a day ago I ran out of after seeing Jezebel. Looking at the room now, I'm surprised to find a brand-new mattress where the old one was, along with a comforter still in its packaging.

"You got a new mattress?" Turning to face Beast, my brow furrowing in confusion. Why would he do something like that?

"Yeah, not about to let you sleep on the other one," he answers, and I get what he's not saying. The mattress he fucked whores and other women on.

"Why?" I cock my head, unable to understand fully.

"Because you're my woman and deserve the respect of knowing the bed you sleep on isn't the same one I used to fuck other women on." His answer's blunt and to the point, just as he is.

Letting my hand go, he steps away.

"We're going to be leaving here soon." I open my mouth to ask him what he means, but he keeps talking. "You're going to stay here at the clubhouse while we're gone. I want you to stick close to the other ol' ladies. Keep safe while I'm gone."

"Where are you going?" I whisper, feeling antsy.

"My brothers and me are going to finish this so I know you're safe. I'm not telling you what we're doing, but you need to trust me on this. I know what I'm doing. The club is handling this situation."

That feeling in my stomach increases, and I want nothing more than to beg him to tell me what they're planning on doing. Instead, I nod in understanding because I know, in the end, he's not going to tell me.

Beast draws me back into his arms and sighs, cupping the back of my head. "It won't take too long, baby. When we get back, you and me, we're going home."

"Okay," I whisper, my breath hitching. "Can someone go get Jagger and bring him here until we do go home? I don't want him there alone for longer than he has to be. He's still a baby."

"I'll get a prospect to go over there and get him for you," Beast agrees, pressing his lips to mine, tongue sliding in to tangle with mine.

Beast keeps the kiss gentle and sweet. Soft and slow. Not in any rush to pull away or take it further, and it scares me because he's never once kissed me like this before.

I moan in protest when he pulls away, going on my tiptoes following him, not ready for him to stop kissing me.

"When I get back, we'll finish this," he says, reaching up to cup the side of my face, his thumb stroking my bottom lip. "Regardless, I get back early or late, we're staying here for a few days. Make sure everything's good before going home."

"Okay," I breathe, a sense of unease filling my stomach. I don't want something to happen to him or anyone else. "Please be careful."

"Plan on it, Butterfingers." Dipping his head down, Beast kisses me once more, drops his hand, and takes mine in his in order for us to go back to the main room.

A thought crosses my mind, and I stop just before we leave the room. "I don't have any clothes here."

"Yeah, you do, baby. I brought them a few days ago and put them in the dresser." He surprised me with his answer.

How had I not noticed any of my clothes were missing?

"You packed some of my clothes from the house and brought them here?" I ask, looking to him for confirmation.

"No, I bought you a few things and put them in the dresser." He grins. "There's those yoga leggings you like to wear, the tank tops, and a couple pairs of jeans. I think a bra or two and some socks."

"Well, you thought of everything but panties, didn't you?" I huff, rolling my eyes.

"I'd say I did. Now, come on, baby, let's get back to the front so I can get with my brothers and head out. The sooner I get this shit done, the faster it'll be for me to get back home to you."

Nodding, I walk with him toward the front of the clubhouse and find all the ol' ladies are already congregated in one area, my sister with them.

"Are the kids all in the playroom?" I ask no one in particular when I make it to them, Beast behind me.

"Yeah," Ivy answers, grinning. "They're watching *Wednesday* because Sage demanded it, and you know Reaper gives into his little girl."

"Oh, I know." I can't help but giggle, feeling for the other kids. Sage is definitely into that show and *The Addams Family* movies.

"I'll go sit with them," Giselle announces. "I haven't seen it yet, and I really wanted to."

"Okay." Ivy nods. "If they start getting on your nerves, come back and join us."

No one speaks another word as she leaves the room. I get the feeling that though she likes being around the other women, she prefers the children right now. I can't blame her there.

Beast wraps his arms around my waist from behind. "We're heading out. If you need me, call. Cerberus and Azrael are staying here with Serpent and

Ghost. Gizmo and Minion are going to go pick up Jagger and get some stuff for him to bring here."

"Okay," I murmur, twisting in his hold to face him. "I'll see you when you get back."

Tilting my head back enough, I let out a sigh when he dips down and kisses me briefly.

"Stay in the clubhouse," he orders as he lets me go and stalks off toward his brothers.

That sense of unease doesn't go away, and I want nothing more than to call Beast's name and tell him not to leave me.

I even open my mouth to do just that but stop myself. He doesn't need me to freak out on him and demand he not leave me behind. Instead, I clamp my mouth shut and watch him as he goes through the door.

No sooner the door closes behind them all, a loud explosion fills the air and causes all of us in the room to jump as it rocks the building. There's not a chance for any of us to do more than that before the world comes crashing down around me.

Something heavy hits me, and I barely register anything but the ringing in my ears and the sound of screams and crying of my friends. It's all I can do to keep from letting myself be dragged down into the depths of unconsciousness. Through the ringing, I can somewhat hear the sounds of men and, if I'm not mistaken, Beast calling my name.

But I'm sure it's wishful thinking. That first explosion had to have been for the guys, though I'm not completely certain. Everything hurts, and I'm fighting to stay awake. To stay fighting. The others . . . they need me. I need to help them. If only I could move. I would do just that. Unfortunately, I can feel myself being pulled under, unconsciousness taking hold.

The last thing I comprehend is yet another explosion. I only wish that no one else is hurt.

CHAPTER 20

BEAST

The explosion hit hard, and none of us could have seen it coming. My only thought was getting to Bristol, her and the others. The first explosion set us all flying backward having missed us, but instead took out our bikes. The next one is the one that got us through. Not us exactly, but the women. It hit the front of the clubhouse, taking it out.

Rushing through the debris, I search for Bristol and the others. I have a general idea of where they were before the explosion.

"Reaper," Ivy screams, stumbling to her feet, dust coating her face, tears streaming down her cheeks, and blood marring her forehead. "Paxton and Sage!"

"You take care of them," Azrael yells out. "We'll go check on the kids."

"I'm with him," Cerberus shouts, following behind them.

"Same here," Ghost grunts, rushing past me. "We'll get the kids out."

"Take them through the back, get them to my house," Reaper orders.

I tune everyone else out while moving through the room, searching for Bristol.

Making it to the last spot I saw her, I started removing debris out of the way. There's concrete, brick, and metal all around. Diablo and two others start helping me lift the broken pieces. After what feels like forever, my heart racing in my chest, I not only find her but get her out.

"Get her to the back. We'll check her over there," Thanatos shouts from where he's helping Tombstone with Sutton.

I don't say anything. I couldn't, even if I thought I could. My focus is on Bristol and her unconscious form in my arms.

"We're moving everyone to Prez's house," Scythe states, his woman in his arms as well.

"We'll get everyone there then see to wounds and shit," Reaper declares, Ivy tucked to his side. "We need to know what the fuck happened here."

My mind whirls back to what Jezebel said when Azrael and Cerberus dragged her into church and the warning she gave.

Fuck.

This has to be what she was talking about. But who could be behind it? The Scarlet Needles? My family? Bristol's?

None of this is sitting well with me. Something's coming and I don't like the feeling clenching at my gut.

The only thing that makes sense to me is the possibility that it's my family. There's no way the Scarlet Needles would take out the women they've put a contract on that they want. The Swedish relatives . . . they have the means and wouldn't even blink in order to do something like this.

First things first, see to Bristol then handle the rest. I'm not about to let them get away with this. I'll kill them all. They want me in their midst, then so fucking be it. I'll go to them if only to kill them with my bare hands.

"We need to get Bristol to the hospital," Stella announces, wiping her hands over her face in frustration.

"It's not secure to take her there," Reaper remarks,

his daughter in one arm, his son curled around a leg, and his woman tucked into his side. "Can you take care of her here?"

"No, she could possibly have internal bleeding, and if I don't get her there, it could end up killing her." Stella keeps her voice calm, not frightening the children sitting around the room, all of them scared.

"She could die?" Giselle whispers, and something flickers in her gaze. "She can't die."

"I'm not going to let that happen. But in order to see to that, I need to have her at the hospital," Stella says, looking at me. "If you don't want to lose her, we need to move."

I nod and scoop my woman back in my arms. My mind's sole focus right now is making sure she gets the care she needs.

"I'm coming with you," Giselle announces.

"You should stay here," I grumble.

"She's my sister, and I'm not staying behind," the other woman snaps, moving to my side.

"I don't care who is going and who's not, but we need to go," Stella states sternly and looks to her ol' man. "I know you're coming with me."

"Fuck yeah, I am. Sutton and the other ol' ladies are going to watch after our boy," Angel remarks, nostrils flaring.

"Good, then you can drive while I help Beast with

Bristol and call into the hospital to have a gurney ready upon us getting there."

I block out the rest of what she says and head for the door, ready to get there and find out if Bristol's okay. Out of all those that had been in the explosion, she's the only one who didn't come out with only a few bruises and scratches.

Getting in the back seat of the SUV, Giselle climbs in the front while Stella slides in next to me.

"When we get there, I'm ordering an MRI and CT scan. I'll also have her arm X-rayed. I don't like the way it looks. Is there a possibility that she's pregnant, Beast?" Stella asks while checking Bristol's pulse once again.

"There's a chance," I answer, not wanting to think of the possibility right now. "She's not on birth control."

"And you guys never seem to want to use condoms." Stella snorts, shaking her head.

"We always wrapped our shit before getting our ol' ladies," Angel states mockingly.

"Yeah, yeah, just hurry and get us to the hospital. I don't like how weak Bristol's pulse is."

Those words rip into my soul. I can't lose her. Not now. Not fucking ever.

In no time, Angel's got us pulling into the ambulance entrance and Stella hops out. I follow right behind her as two nurses come out with the gurney.

Orders were made as I lay Bristol down, and she's rushed away. As much as I want to follow, I'm not stupid. Stella's with her, and she'll make sure nothing happens to my woman.

I turn to face my VP, only to find myself facing Giselle. However, the look in her eye isn't the one I've seen her to have since we first rescued her. It's one that matches her mother's, and I realize something I should have known all along. She's in on whatever is going on here.

"What's going on?" I ask, furrowing a brow.

"You ruined everything," she snaps. "Everything."

"What did I ruin?" I cock my head, not liking the fact that behind her in the driver's seat, Angel hasn't moved. "What did you do to Angel?"

"Exactly what he deserved. What all of you deserve," she states, stepping into my space. The tip of something in her hand presses into my stomach. "You couldn't just stay away from Bristol, let my mother have what she wanted from her. Let them take her and do what they want to do."

"Are you even pregnant?" I find myself asking, seeing her for the first time, and what type of person she really is.

"If I were, I'd abort it in a heartbeat, and Ronnie

knows it," she scoffs. "Now, get in the front seat with your dead friend there. We'll make this quick, and I'll be on my way."

"You think I'm that stupid?" There's no way I'm going to do anything this bitch says. Behind her on the driver's side, I note the slightest movement from Angel and know he's not dead as Giselle seems to think he is. "Got to say you might be the dumbest bitch I know to pull something like this off right outside a hospital. You realize they've got cameras, right?"

"I know what I'm doing," Giselle snaps, sneering at me. "Now, do as I told you."

"First, answer me this. You're planning on killing me, so who was behind the bombing with you?" I want to know who I need to kill when this bullshit is over with.

"That would be Cordell and his contact within the Scarlet Needles. He went to your cousins first, but they didn't want any part in this. Evidently, they've grown tired of the feud after your mother's death and are wiping their hands of the lot of you. Cordell thought it would be easy enough to frame them when we went after Bristol."

"You want her for what purpose?"

"It's obvious, isn't it?" Giselle smirks. "Her money. The investments. Everything that was left to her and should have been mine." Yeah, this bitch has lost it.

"Enough of this. Now, get in the SUV so I can get this done and out of here."

"I think I'm good here," I state and move quickly as Angel points his gun and shoots Giselle from behind. It's not what either of us would have wanted but we know the truth now. There's nothing else we could have found out from the bitch. She gave us all she had, and I'd bet money on it.

Moving quickly to the driver's side door, I throw the door open to assess Angel's wounds.

"Fuckin' bitch tried to kill me," he rasps.

"Good thing we're right outside the hospital," I quip. "Stella is going to be pissed you've gotten yourself stabbed."

"Don't I fuckin' know it," Angel grunts while I help him get out. As sirens ring out, police cars pull in along with two other SUVs, with my brothers coming up behind. It sucks all of our bikes are gone, but they can be replaced.

"Come on, VP, let's get you inside and patched up." Helping him toward the doors, we're again met by nurses who take him back. Security steps in front of me and ushers me back out.

I know I'm going to have to deal with the cops and fill in my brothers on what the fuck just happened here.

Reaper and Officer Bryant meet me right outside the doors.

"Angel okay?" Reaper demands.

"He will be," I answer and nod toward Giselle's body on the ground. "She fooled us all." Quickly, I explain everything she said to both men and let out a heavy breath.

"I've already got officers picking them all up. Scythe has footage of them and two other men who were a part of the explosion at the clubhouse. We'll go over the video footage from here, and it'll all be handled," Bryant explains.

"It can't be that easy for this to be done," I remark, shaking my head.

"Normally, it wouldn't be, but before you all were attacked, Bristol's father and brother were also hit. They're okay but knew who was behind it when it happened. We were already on to them when you were hit. We were just too late to be of help, and I apologize for that." You could hear the sincerity in the other man's voice.

"It's done now. Can we go in and find out about my brother and his woman?" Reaper demands, his voice thick with rage.

"Yeah, if we need anything else, I know where to find you," Bryant says. He steps away, turns, and heads toward a few other officers.

"Come on, you can tell me what you didn't tell us when we get to the others. We left the prospects at my house with all the women."

I nod in response to Reaper's order. "First, can we find out how Bristol's doing, then I'll tell you all." I nearly lost her, and I know when she finds out what happened here and who was behind the bombing of the clubhouse, it's going to destroy her.

"Yeah, I want to know myself how she's doing." Reaper grunts, clasps a hand on my shoulder, and meets my gaze with his hard ones. "This is over for her, and she doesn't need to know the details of everything."

"Can't keep this from her, Prez." I shake my head. "She's going to question why Angel killed her sister. She thought they were finally going to have a relationship. It's going to devastate her to find out what really happened and why."

"You're right it will." Reaper nods, rolls his shoulders, and lets go of my shoulder before heading in the direction of our brothers.

Together, we all head into the waiting room to find out about my woman and our VP.

Six hours later and with a few more questions from the police, Stella finally emerges from behind the doors to the back.

"How's Bristol?" I ask, not waiting around.

"As I thought earlier, Bristol does indeed have a concussion. Her wrist is broken, we had to go in and repair it. She also has a few broken ribs, which I'm sure is due to the debris she was buried under. Overall, she was lucky it didn't puncture a lung. We also had to go in and remove her spleen." Stella goes on to explain what they were doing for her now and that she should soon be in a room rather than recovery. Turning to Reaper, she narrowed her gaze. "My husband, on the other hand, is already in a room and knows I'm not pleased with him." Again, she goes over the details of what they've had to do for him by going in and repairing the damage Giselle did to him with that knife of hers. "Now, I'm going to go back to Angel's room because I'm tired and exhausted. You can send someone to get me a tea and meal from Spuds."

"You got it," Reaper remarks. "I'll be up soon as I call and check in with Ivy." He hadn't let any of the ol' ladies come up here after what went down. He even sent Styxx and Diablo back to his house to watch over them.

Stella nods and leaves the way she came.

I turn toward my brothers and wait for whatever

Reaper's going to say.

Glancing around at each of us, he murmured the words I knew were coming. "Those three might be in custody, but there's more to this. We all know it. The Scarlet Needles are behind this in some way, shape or form, and I'm sick of it. This is the final straw. They want a war, they've got it. Anyone object?"

"With you," I growl, more than ready to go after them. To spill their blood for once.

Each of my brothers that are here make their agreements known, and Reaper nods.

"Good, let's get Bristol and Angel out of here and healed. Until then, we'll rebuild the clubhouse and start planning," Reaper remarks.

"Quick question," Tombstone says gruffly. "What the fuck are we going to do with the bitch we had taken to the cabin?"

"Harvester and Thanatos, you two can take care of her. Find out if there's anything else she might know, then discard her body where she'll never be found," Reaper orders, turns, and starts toward the elevator, done with the conversation.

"Find out if she has anything else to say about my Swedish relatives or if it was all Cordell giving her the ammo she needed to get under our skin," I mutter and also head for the elevator, more than ready to see my woman, and to know that she's okay.

CHAPTER 21

BRISTOL

The first thing that I realize when I come to is that I'm in the hospital and can hear Beast talking softly to me. My body hurts. I don't think there's a part of me that doesn't feel a bit of pain.

Memories come back to me about what happened, and panic starts to seep in. Is everyone okay? Was anyone else hurt? Beast was out there with the first explosion.

"Sheesh, Butterfingers, you're okay," Beast murmurs, having picked up on the fact I'm awake, though I haven't opened my eyes yet.

Slowly, I peek through my lower lashes to meet Beast's dark gaze. I notice immediately that we're not alone. Not far behind him is my brother, and on the other side of the bed sits my dad.

"What are you doing here?" I croak, my throat dry, and it feels like razor blades were in it.

"Here, baby, drink this," Beast says, holding a small cup with the straw pointed at my lips. "You've been asleep for the past three days."

Three days.

Oh God.

"Was anyone else hurt?" I whisper, finishing taking a couple sips, unable to get the thought out of my head.

"Just some bumps and bruises," Beast answers, setting the cup back down, his eyes never leaving me. "But I'm not going to lie to you because you have the right to know. Giselle is dead."

"What?" I barely get the word out as I find it hard to believe.

"She tricked you, Bristol." It's my dad who answers, getting my attention, and I see the pain in his features. "She and your mother were in on whatever they were trying to do. To get to you and try to drive you away so they could find a way to control you, they set this all up. Giselle stabbed one of the members of the club and was going to kill Beast." Shaking his head, he closes his eyes. "I'm sorry, sweetheart, but it's over now."

"She tricked me?" A part of me doesn't want to believe it, but another does. She was always close to my mom. Some would say thick as thieves.

God, how could I be so foolishly blind?

Tears prick my eyes, and I suck in a breath to keep them from shedding. I won't cry, not for her.

"This is all my fault," I whisper, my thoughts going to the very fact that this all happened to the club because of me.

"Don't even think that shit, baby," Beast remarks harshly. "This isn't on you, and no one blames you."

"But . . ."

Beast leans in, getting nose to nose with me. "You are not to blame for this shit, so get the thought out of your head."

I take in the tone of his voice and nod. Granted, I still feel it and will apologize to the others later. For now, I'll drop it.

"Now, someone's going to get the doctor so we can make sure you're okay," Beast states, looking over his shoulder to my brother.

Closing my eyes, I relax in the hospital bed, wishing I were home with Jagger. Without opening my eyes, I whisper, "Jagger."

"He's at Reaper's. Paxton and Sage are loving up on him."

That's good.

My poor cat must think I've abandoned him.

"When we get you out of here, we'll be staying at Reaper and Ivy's until you're well enough to go home. He'll be waiting for you when we get there." Beast must've sensed my thoughts because those words eased a part of me.

"Okay," I utter, feeling myself growing exhausted. "I think I'm going back to sleep now."

"Rest, Butterfingers," he murmurs and presses a kiss to the back of my hand with the IV.

I should ask him why my other hand is in a cast, but I don't. It's not something I want to know at the moment. That can come later, when I'm not so tired.

"I want to go home, I'm tired of being in here," I proclaim two days later, glaring at Beast.

"Baby, you'll go when they say you can," he remarks, a slight smirk curving on his lips.

"They can release me. All I'm doing is lying here, watching mindless TV and reading trashy magazines. I don't have anything new on my Kindle to read, and I don't want to do any rereads right now." Huffing, I wish I could just get up and go, but Beast won't allow it.

"Bristol, you need to be patient."

"Screw patient. I want to go home."

"Let's see what the doctor says when she comes in. How's that?" he offers.

"I guess." Shrugging, I roll my head against the pillow.

My body still hurts really bad, but I can handle it better if I wasn't going stir-crazy being in this hospital room. I want to go home, or at least to Reaper and Ivy's house, where I can get in my old bed and curl up with Jagger while Beast holds me.

Beast moves into my line of view and leans in bracing hands on each side of my waist, taking care not to hurt me in any way. "I know you want out of here as fast as you can, but for me, baby, let them do their job in taking care of you. If something were to go wrong, I'd lose my shit because I can't lose you."

"Beast." His name comes out no more than a whisper.

"Listen to me, Bristol," he commands gently. "We dug you out of the debris. I didn't know if you were okay or not. I carried you out of there. We brought you to the hospital, and I didn't know if you were going to be okay or not. I need you to be okay, so please don't argue about this."

My chest tightens, and I lick my lips while nodding. "I love you."

"Love you too, Butterfingers, and I swear the

moment you're out of here and healed up, I'm marrying you. I'm not about to let you go. Not again. Not ever."

"Is this your way of asking me to marry you?" I can't help but giggle.

"Damn right, it is." Beast presses a tender kiss to my lips.

"Then it's a good thing I have no problem with saying yes or holding on to you as you hold me."

I don't know what else is going to happen. I know it's not over with. Not when it comes to the Scarlet Needles. Beast told me what he could about it all, and it's scary to think about, but I trust him and the others to protect us all. He'll do whatever it takes to see to my safety. I'll hold on to him to make sure he stays alive to have a future with me so I won't ever be without him again.

BONUS SCENE

DIABLO

Six months.

That's how long it's been since the club was attacked, and we nearly lost my brother's woman. It's a damn good thing Beast didn't lose her, though otherwise, we would have lost him as well. Seeing the love between the two of them, knowing Bristol has given my brother what he's needed for as long as I've known him, opens something inside me that I thought was dead all this time.

With the clubhouse now rebuilt, we've upped the security and remodeled what needed to be done. The ol' ladies were happy about it since they got to upgrade the kitchen and get new furnishings for the main room.

At the same time, we've also been doing a shit ton to take on the Scarlet Needles. One of those things is we've questioned Jezebel and used everything we could to ensure she didn't hide anything else from us. It's a good thing for her because we ended up letting her live. Though she's still being housed in the cabin secured where no one can find her.

Because of her and what Giselle informed us, we were able to confirm Beast's Swedish family had nothing to do with anything and that she was to fool him into thinking it was them behind everything. Cordell seemed to want Beast out of the way. For what, I don't know for sure, but I know it's more than just the money Bristol has in her name and trust.

But what no one knows is the shit that's also been going on with me that I haven't talked about. Not even with Beast. He's got enough on his plate with Bristol.

No, what I've got needs to be handled personally without my brothers. If it's not, then there's more of a chance I could lose everything I finally have in my life. Then again, with my brothers, it might be easier, but I could end up losing everything.

It's a gamble I'm not sure if I'm ready to take. However, it's one I'll have to take regardless.

There is a life at stake here. Not mine or anyone in the club, but someone, rather the only woman who's ever touched me a way that rocked my world. Back then, she wasn't a woman but just a girl who needed to be protected. She ran away long ago from a life she knew, only to be sent back to it. Now, she's disappeared altogether, and I'm going to have to find her.

And do it before it's too late.

If this is the first book you're reading by E.C. Land. Be sure to check out where she started it all with Horse's Bride.

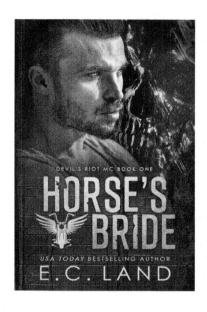

CHAPTER 1

HORSE

It's fucking early as hell out, but I can't help that I love the open road, the smell of the fresh air, and the feel of my bike under me as I'm riding. Riding out this morning seeing the sunrise as we make our way out of the national charter's clubhouse lot has to be one of the most amazing sights I've ever seen. Almost as if it were a sign of the things to come as we head toward the new clubhouse that we're expanding.

I feel a calm being out on the open road on my girl, feeling the power she brings me as we make our way on the interstate. Knowing she's the only girl in my life that won't ever fail me no matter the situation we find ourselves in. I can always count on her handling whatever comes our way.

Twister who is Prez of the Devils Riot's new charter, as well as my best friend, rides next to me heading toward our new location. The brothers had made the decision in our last church session to expand the club with a new charter. Granted there are already several charters up and down the East Coast as well as some going toward the Midwest. Our farthest charter is out in Colorado. With us moving to this location it will be the closest charter to any of the docks we deal with. The Russians that we work with are known for dealing in guns and the docks out here are a lot easier to use than most. Less conspicuous. With us moving to the new clubhouse we have fifteen guys and four prospects. Today it's just Twister, Rage, Thorn, and I riding out. The others will be coming tomorrow.

We want to get a good look around and start making a list of all the shit that needs to be done staking out our new territory. Easier to do when it's just four guys instead of the whole club around. When you have a shit ton of brothers walking around the same area it's fucking hard to see everything that needs to get done.

I need gas and to piss, so I signal the Prez by tapping the side of my leg to get his attention so he'll pull up to the next gas station we see. He nods as we see a sign for the next station coming up in two miles. Damn, I've been on the road so many times on runs,

I've forgotten how bad it is when you've had shit sleep. Lucky for me, cause I really need coffee and aspirin. Twister had wanted to get on the road before dawn this morning so that we can be there before lunch. We had a huge ass bash last night, and the club pussy was thrown our way. Swear all the girls wanted to take a turn with us. I took three of them back to my room, and watched as they took turns sucking me off until I painted their faces with my cum. The fun part was while I had one riding my face, and one on my dick the other would be sucking my nuts or licking her friend's clit. Fuck I've been tired, but never exhausted as I was this morning when I got up.

"Why did we have to leave so fucking early again? Couldn't you have picked a better time to leave than the ass crack of dawn?"

I grumble to Twister as we park our bikes next to the gas pumps. Rage and Thorn both shake their heads, just as tired as I am. Yeah, I'll crash when we get to Twister's sister's house. Not knowing what shape the new clubhouse is in, it makes sense to crash at his sister's for now. All our shit is still back in Stonewall Mills. I'm not going to sleep on the damn floor or pay for a room if I don't have to. Only thing I know about the new clubhouse is that Twister and Stoney, our national Prez, picked it out and had it designed and built for the most part. We're supposed to do the rest.

Something tells me there's a lot of clean up. Since all our shit won't be here until later this week when the rest of the guys show up, we needed a place to crash. No reason to pay for rooms at a motel or sleep on the floor of the clubhouse when his sister lives so close.

Twister turns toward me smirking with a knowing look. "Quit your bitching and shut the fuck up, Horse. You can sleep when you're fucking dead." He says trying to be serious.

I shake my head. "You know I ain't a morning person especially without coffee in my veins."

"Ain't that the fucking truth." He starts laughing. "No fucker, I wanted to head out early so I can surprise my sis with lunch before she heads to work. If I can't catch her before work, I'm hoping to catch her before she gets busy."

Chuckling, I look at him "Why didn't you just say that shit in the first fucking place? Didn't know you were that wrapped around your sister's pinky."

Shaking his head, he grumbles, "I haven't seen her since her birthday a year ago. I've barely had time to talk to her on the phone with all the shit we have going on with the move and all."

Yeah Twister's a sucker for his sister. Never met the chick but I have respect for her from everything that he's said about her. Especially since she's his only blood relative left. The Bastards Sons took out his dad, and his mom ran out on his sister and him when Twister was seventeen. It left him to take care of his kid sister. His bitch of a mom didn't even bother to explain why she left them, just fucking took off leaving them to fend for themselves. I guess shit moms don't bother explaining though. Twister stepped up big time while prospecting for Devils Riot. He always made sure his sister was taken care of, being the only male figure in her life. When any of the guys asked about his sister, Twister would go fucking ballistic not wanting anyone to fuck with her, his brothers included.

"So, what's your sister's name anyway?" I ask, fishing for info.

Granted I've never seen her. He doesn't bring her to the club. Evidently, she's been living over four hours away from him for a while now. I wonder why that is. He never brought her around the club before she moved. One day she just up and left without telling her brother.

Twister hangs up the gas pump eyeing me skeptically. "Her name's Kenny."

I freeze. It's an unusual name for a chick and my luck couldn't be that good or bad.

Not many girls out there named Kenny though.

It couldn't be the same girl, Kenny was a sweet ass, and I was her first without even realizing it. I can still remember everything about her body.

Four Years Ago

Dammit, I hate when I gotta go anywhere close to a store that doesn't have anything to do with bike parts. Now that's something I can do but going to the damn grocery store to get shit for the clubhouse? That's a job for the prospects and club whores. I shouldn't be the one going into a damn grocery store. Definitely shouldn't have pissed off the VP last night by trying to hit on his latest piece of ass.

Shaking my head as I make my way into the store, I stop dead in my tracks when I spot the hottest body I've ever seen in my life. Tight jeans covering a perfect ass with flip flops and a tank top containing the most gorgeous tits I've ever seen. Across her pale shoulders ran a colored tattoo of two dragons intertwined around each other, extending to each other across her shoulder blades. The best part of the dragons would have to be their eyes: one with an aquamarine color, the other with a ruby tint. Between the two dragons, knelt a naked fairy looking upward at the two of them with her arms extended toward their faces. I liked it at first glance, but seeing it in detail I think it's sick.

"That's one wicked-ass tat you got, babe. Where'd you get it done?" *I stop behind her, waiting for her to turn around and hoping that her front end matches her back.*

"Thanks. Ink Masters in Blacksburg," *she mumbles,*

keeping her head down as she scuffles through her purse, not looking up at me like I was hoping she'd do.

"No problem. You got a name?" I shoot her another grin while I wait for her to look up at me.

"Kenny." She finally turns around and my heart almost comes out of my chest. Her eyes had to be the most spectacular blue I've ever seen. They paired perfectly with the dirty blond hair piled up on her head. She was the most exquisite woman I had ever set my eyes on.

"So, how about you and I get out of here and go grab a beer or something." I wouldn't mind getting between those legs of hers instead of having a beer but something about her doesn't make me mind waiting. She looks like she'd be worth it. I can already picture her name spilling off my lips while I drive deep into her.

Yep, I could see that happening.

She smiles at me with plush lips "Sure, I could use a beer."

And I could use that sweet body under me as I come all over those flawless tits. I wonder how I've never seen her before.

"Alright, sweet girl let's get moving then."

That had been the beginning of an impeccable week with Kenny and one that has stuck with me since.

Problem is, I still dream of her anytime I fall asleep, no matter if I'm sober or not.

I shake my head, ridding it of the memory that started it all. It can't be the same chick, it can't be. I can only hope to God that it's not. I know my best friend would kill me if he finds out I touched his sister. It's been unspoken, but we've always known that his sister is off limits. It's club code.

"You ready to get back on the road?" Twister asks. At my nod, he yells out to let the rest of the boys know it's time to get back on the road.

Pulling out of the station and riding next to my Prez and best friend, I feel my mind running a mile a minute. All I can think about is could this be the same Kenny who has been haunting me for the past four years. The woman who I picture every time I fuck some random bitch. The woman that in a week's time, stole my heart and never turned back. The woman I haven't been able to find since I realized she was gone. I swear to fuckin' God if it is, I'll be happy as fuck. I'm also going to be in deep shit.

ALSO BY E.C. LAND

Devil's Riot MC

Horse's Bride

Thorn's Revenge

Twister's Survival

Reclaimed (Devil's Riot MC Boxset Bks 1 – 3)

Cleo's Rage

Connors' Devils

Hades Pain

Badger's Claim

Burner's Absolution

Redeemed (Devil's Riot MC Boxset Bks 4 – 6)

K-9's Fight

Revived Boxset (Devil's Riot MC Boxset Bks 7 — 9)

Red's Calm

Brass's Surrender

Devil's Riot MC Originals

Stoney's Property

Owning Victoria

Blaze's Mark

Taming Coyote

Luna's Shadow

Devil's Ride (DRMC Boxset 1 – 5)

Choosing Nerd

Stoney's Gift

Ranger's Fury

Carrying Blaze's Mark

Neo's Strength

Cane's Dominance

Venom's Prize

Protecting Blaze's Mark

Devil's Reign (DRMC Boxset 6 – 10)

Whip's Breath

Viper's Touch

Cyprus's Truth

<u>Devil's Riot MC Southeast</u>

Hammer's Pride

Malice's Soul

Axe's Devotion

Ruin Boxset 1 – 3

Rebelling Rogue

Remaining Gunner's

Savage's Honor

Revenge Boxset 4 – 6

Devil's Riot MC Tennessee

Breaking Storm

Blow's Smoke

Nines's Time

Lucky's Streak

Defiance Boxset 0.5 – 3

Devil's Riot MC Mississippi

Fighting Rosemary

Inferno's Clutch MC

Chains' Trust

Breaker's Fuse

Ryder's Rush

Axel's Promise

Fated for Pitch Black

Their Redemption Boxset 1 - 5

Tiny's Hope

Fuse's Hold

Nora's Outrage

Tyres' Wraith

Brielle's Nightmare

Their Salvation Boxset 6 - 10

Pipe's Burn

Faith's Tears

Lyrica's Lasting

Brake's Intent

Speed's Ride

Dark Lullabies

A Demon's Sorrow

A Demon's Bliss

A Demon's Harmony

A Demon's Soul

A Demon's Song

Dark Lullabies Boxset

Royal Bastards MC (Elizabeth City Charter)

Cyclone of Chaos

Spiral into Chaos

Aligned Hearts

Embraced

Entwined

Entangled

Crush Boxset 1-3

Ensnared

Entrapped

Night's Bliss

Finley's Adoration (Co-Write with Elizabeth Knox)

Cedric's Ecstasy

Arwen's Rapture

Christmas Delight

Satan's Keepers MC

Keeping Reaper

Forever Tombstone's

Hellhound's Sacrifice

Outrage Boxset 1 – 3

Mercy's Angel

Facing Daemon

Scythe's Grasp

Mayhem Boxset 4 – 6

Holding Beast

Toxic Warriors MC

Viking

Ice

War

Storm Boxset 1 – 3

Grimm

Maverick

De Luca Crime Family

Frozen Valentine (Prequel)

Frozen Kiss

Heated Caress

Simmering Embrace

Scorched Boxset (1 – 3)

Fiery Affection

Inflamed Touch

Sons of Norhill Tops

Inheriting Trouble

Dancing Struggles

Burning Tears

Pins and Needles Series

Blood and Agony

Blood and Torment

Blood and Betrayal

Agony Boxset 1 - 3

DeLancy Crime Family

Degrade

Deprave

Detest

Desire Boxset 1 - 3

Deny

Demean

Delusion

Destroy Boxset 4 - 6

Underground Bruisers with Rae B. Lake

Caging Dyer

Finding Reese

Breaking Phoenix

Available on Audible

Reclaimed

Cleo's Rage

Connors' Devils

Hades Pain

Badger's Claim

Dear Readers,

I hope you all have enjoyed reading Holding Beast. I'm sure it's left you with a few questions about what's going to happen next. Touching Diablo is the next book to Satan's Keepers MC and I have to say Diablo is going to be one man no one wants to mess with.

Sincerely,
 E.C.

Corbin's Conflict

*This life is a choice. One you make
with or without confliction.*

CORBIN

Things are happening in my town and my county. We're split between two clubs. Rivals that share blood and a common enemy.

Witches.

I hate them. All of them. I have my reasons, but fate seems to have other plans. Plans I don't care much for.

The day she comes into my life, I want to throw the raven-haired, emerald-eyed beauty out, but she can help in ways we need. The question is, can I resist the bond between us when the heat grows hot?

Danger swirls around us and we're left with no other choice but to trust one another. Conflicted, I decide to let my instincts lead, even when that decision puts her in my arms.

Lynch's Match

Once burned the pain is all that's left.

LYNCH

The past is finally come to the present and nothing else can stop the anger building inside me. She was supposed to be my match. The one person who was always mine and mine alone, but that was a lie.

Now she's back in town and I didn't even know it until it was too late. She's going to get herself killed if I don't do something about it first.

With the past always comes the demons and they seem to have targeted her. This is something I won't allow. To protect her, I'll keep her close. Make sure nothing happens to her. Keep the monsters away from her.

However, I have to do this, it won't be easy. She's still my match. The one woman meant for me, but that doesn't mean I have anything to offer her. Nothing more than my protection.

Or does it?

Shiner's Light

A light only shines bright for as long as it's lit. The dark is always threatening to extinguish it.

SHINER

The only things that matter to me in this world are my boy and my club. I don't need anything else. Don't want it. I'm happy with the way my life is. At least, that's what I thought, until she popped back into my life.

She vanished years ago, and I didn't think I'd ever see her again. Now, she's asking for help, and I want to turn her away, but she's my son's family, the only one who cared anything for him. Can I just walk away, or do I try to reignite the light that used to make her shine?

Stiker's Yield

Life has a way of making you yield, but it won't stop me from getting what I want most.

STRIKER

The first time I saw her, I knew she was pure. Sweet and shy, it works for her. She's not the type I usually go for, but that didn't stop me from wanting her.

She didn't come around often, so it was easy for me to ignore her. Until I couldn't anymore.

Danger stalks the night and threatens her in a way that draws us in. To protect her, I have to choose, but will I be able to live with it or do I walk?

SOCIAL MEDIA
BE SURE TO FOLLOW OR STALK ME!

Goodreads
Bookbub
DRMC BABES
Instagram
Author Page

Printed in Great Britain
by Amazon